THE DARK ROAD
The Beginning

A NOVELLA

ZACK TOLLIVER, FBI, MYSTERY SERIES

R LAWSON GAMBLE

Special thanks to Super Readers Ann & Craig for above and beyond!

"The road of life stretches out before every human being. The road has many divides. At these divides every human being must choose the light road or the dark road. Sometimes it is hard to see the dark road." Ashkii Nez

CHAPTER ONE

A sudden blast of hot wind set his tie flapping and flew on to form a spiral of dust beyond him on the deserted tarmac. His ears throbbed with the drone of the Cessna 172 he had just deplaned. He stood, suitcase in hand, the solitary vertical object in a horizontal world of runway and sand and watched the small plane inch away raising dust with its single prop. At last it reached the far end of the narrow airstrip and performed a clumsy pirouette, pausing momentarily as if undecided as its engine's roar grew. It surged forward now, accelerated rapidly and somehow, as if by accident, bumped up into the air. Suddenly graceful, it angled southward and soared away joyously, all its former bonds with the clumsy earth now severed. For Zack Tolliver, FBI, it took with it the last vestige of everything he'd known in his short twenty-four years of life.

He watched the black dot fade into the dark blue. Long after it disappeared from his sight and its mechanical drone became one with the wind, he sighed and turned his head in a slow sweeping arc. A flat barren landscape surrounded him, gray and rust-red, defined by faraway vertical cliffs layered with horizontal ledges like a ladder for giants. At his feet, eruptions of yellow-green weed clawed at cracks in the aging concrete of the tarmac. His searching eyes found nothing resembling a terminal.

The enormity of his transforming experience settled upon him like the dust itself, growing in him as the heat of the July afternoon assailed him. An occasional isolated breeze blew even hotter, like a dragon's breath. Sweat appeared in droplets on his brow, neatly trimmed brown hair became plastered to his forehead. The creases in his new polyester-rayon trousers expired, soggy circles bloomed in the armpits of his white linen shirt, his expensively tailored jacket wilted.

Within minutes he removed his jacket, folded it carefully over his arm, relishing the momentary cooling effect of air moving against his damp shirt. He glanced at his watch. Ten minutes had ticked by since he landed. He stood his suitcase on end and sat on it. Another quarter hour passed. He tugged the carefully crafted knot on his tie and opened his collar. The jacket went up above his head to serve as a parasol.

Zachary Efrem Tolliver, newly minted FBI Special Agent just out of the National Academy at Quantico, might as well have been on another planet. He had not asked for this assignment. His instructors at the Academy had noted Zack's unusual empathy for his fellow trainees and how he had assisted those who struggled. He could not have known his posting to the Navajo Nation Reservation was all but decided while he was still a NAT (New Agent Trainee). The FBI Liaison Office of the Criminal Investigative Division, that communication nerve center of ICCU (Indian Country Crimes Unit) struggled to find enough agents willing to partner with reservation law enforcement units nationwide, and, more importantly, to exhibit actual concern for the plight of reservation Indians. Nowhere was such empathy more needed than on the massive Navajo Nation Reservation. Thus, unknown to him, Zack's future had been etched long before his graduation.

Zack was born and raised in Maryland where the longest open expanse was the Chesapeake Bay and the hottest moving air he'd ever experienced was the hand drier in the McDonalds restroom. Regardless, he accepted the assignment eagerly, excited by the idea of exploring a new land, curious to experience the native culture. He had planned to make a strong first impression. That plan was fading fast.

The grind of an engine came to him before he actually saw the truck swimming through the haze of heat at the opposite end of the tarmac. From the sounds it made it needed a valve job. As it drew nearer he saw it needed a paint job as well. Originally red, the truck sported clashing spots of rust and orangish attempts at touchup. It lurched strangely despite the flat surface of the airstrip.

The pickup jerked to a stop next to Zack, the driver's window open despite the heat. The man inside regarded him with squinting brown eyes, the sun-darkened face shadowed by the brim of a wide hat. The man said nothing.

"I'm waiting for my ride," Zack said, feeling he needed to explain. "It should be here any moment."

"Get in," the man said.

Zack stared. The man had the classic features of every Indian he had ever seen on TV, particularly the bad ones. "No, thanks. My ride is coming."

"This is it."

"I'm to be picked up by Agent Ben Brewster."

"This is it."

"Are you saying Agent Brewster sent you?"

The driver raised an eyebrow a millimeter, refusing to explain the situation yet one more time.

Zack picked up his suitcase.

"Throw it in the back," the man said.

Zack walked to the rear of the truck and lifted the suitcase over the tailgate onto the bed, placing it as far away as possible from the smeared gas can and oil-covered rope. At his first try, the passenger door wouldn't open. He pulled harder and it gave with a groan and dropped an inch as it swung wide. He glanced in at the driver, who was facing stoically forward, and climbed in avoiding the worst of the torn upholstery. He placed a polished shoe either side of the gallon water bottles at his feet. It took both hands to close the door. The latch did not sound convincing.

They lurched off without a word. Zack's eye wandered the cab interior. Roof liner hung, a crack in the cab's rear window resembled a huge spider web, a coffin-like crate containing chains and large hooks and several boxes of what appeared to be ammunition was squeezed into the area behind the seat. A gun rack held a single rifle. The weapon seemed to be the only item in the truck treated with any kind of care.

"My name is Zack Tolliver," he said, filling the silence.

"I know."

"Thank you for the ride."

The man glanced at him. "You are here to help Ben Brewster."

It might have been a question or a statement. Zack wasn't sure. He nodded.

"I am glad. Ben is a good man," the driver said.

From the smooth tarmac they rolled onto a dirt track where the truck rocked and rattled. Dust floated into the cab through the open windows. After half a mile they came to a paved two-lane road where the driver coaxed the old truck to a higher speed. Zack stared through the dusty windshield. The landscape was barren, treeless, wild. Occasional buildings appeared in the distance, far from the road, scattered here and there as if dropped and forgotten, all small houses, usually with junked cars nearby.

No hedges, flowers beds or lawns surrounded them, only a cottonwood tree or two offered shade.

The road unfolded before them like cable off a spool. It rose and knifed through a ridge crest, the cut showing red on each side like a wound. A billboard gave hints of habitation somewhere ahead, but its wording was too weathered to read. They crested a rise. Up ahead a gasoline sign rose above a cluster of buildings.

Zack was relieved to see any sign of civilization. Ever since stepping off the Cessna he'd felt disoriented. The gas station brought a sense of normalcy. And he needed a restroom.

They came to the crossroads and stopped for a red light. A large filling station with convenience store occupied the corner on their right, a McDonalds was close by on the left. Road signs indicated a town was somewhere north of the McDonalds. The light changed. The driver drove straight on. To Zack's chagrin, the crossroads and everything there suggesting civilization faded behind them.

"Wasn't that Tuba City?"

"Yep."

"Isn't the FBI office in Tuba City?"

"Yep."

Zack's body grew tense. It came to him he'd never asked for this man's identification before climbing into the truck.

"Where are we going, then?"

"Elk Wells."

"Why are we going there?"

The Navajo turned his unfathomable gaze on Zack. "Ben Brewster said bring you to him there."

Ben Brewster. Supervisory Special Agent in Charge at the Tuba City office. Zack felt a surge of relief at the sound of his name. Apparently, he was not being kidnapped after all. He opened his mouth to ask about Elk Wells but thought better of it. He didn't want another monosyllabic answer.

The road continued across a panorama of red desert bordered by towering buttes against a blue and endless sky. Zack felt strangely empty as if the vastness of the land threatened to diminish him into nothing. It was dry. The wind rushed through the cab and sucked the moisture from his body.

"There is water at your feet." It was as if the Navajo read his mind.

Grateful, Zack reached down for a bottle, twisted off the cap and gulped down a mouthful. It was beyond tepid, but refreshing. He immediately felt better.

A building came into view, then another. Zack had seen pictures in brochures and articles of the traditional Navajo hogan. He stared, curious. More homes came into view, then a cluster of buildings close together, some with large windows, signage, a real town. The truck slowed and angled into a space in front of a small building next to a white Chevrolet Tahoe with an orange and green official emblem on the door. A sign on the store-front window read Navajo Nation Police.

Zack climbed out of the truck and stretched. He turned to thank the driver but the man was already gone, the office screen door just slapping shut. Not much guidance there. Zack stepped up on the boardwalk, took a deep breath and pulled open the door.

All talk stopped the moment he entered, the only sound the creaking groan of an air conditioner. All faces turned toward him except his driver, busy at the coffee station. A stout Navajo woman sat at a desk near the entrance, a white man with an air of authority was conversing with her. He came over to Zack, hand extended.

"Agent Tolliver?"

Zack shook his hand. "Yes, sir."

"Welcome to Navajo Nation. I am Supervisory Agent in Charge Ben Brewster."

He pointed around the room. "This is Lenana Fitzgerald. She pretty much runs the place. That there is Lané Shorter, tribal policeman. That's Sergeant Jimmy Chaparral. He helps Lenana. And of course you know Eagle Feather." He indicated Zack's driver.

Ben turned to face everyone. "Well, now we have Agent Tolliver, let's get to work. Jimmy, why not take Zachary with you." He looked at Zack. "Do you have a weapon?"

"Yes, sir, it's in my—"

"Great. Go with Jimmy. He'll fill you in on the way." Brewster turned to the man called Lané, a short barrel-chested policeman." Lané, you're with Eagle Feather. Take a rifle. Lenana and I will handle communications from here. Questions?"

The men were already moving. Apparently, operations had previously been discussed.

The man called Jimmy had Zack's elbow. "You're with me." He snatched a wide-brimmed hat from a rack and slapped it on Zack's head. "You'll want that." He led Zack out the back of the office, past a restroom, at which Zack stared longingly and into bright sun. He walked toward a battered dust-covered Bronco. Jimmy gestured Zack to climb into the passenger side. Before he could secure his seatbelt, Jimmy threw the vehicle in reverse in a storm of dust, then accelerated forward through an alley to the street where Eagle Feather's truck was already rattling past headed east.

"My suitcase," Zack said. "My weapon—"

"Don't worry." Jimmy gave him a broad grin. "You're not gonna need it."

CHAPTER TWO

Once beyond the town limits, defined by one or two houses and then nothing, they picked up speed and tried to keep Eagle Feather's truck in view. The roadside brush flashed by in a blur.

"What's going on?" Zack asked.

Jimmy glanced at him. The Navajo policeman was young and slim with pleasant features. His black hair contrasted with pale skin for a Navajo. "We have a hostage situation."

Zack felt an immediate surge of adrenalin. "You said I didn't need my sidearm."

Jimmy grinned. "You don't. You likely won't be involved. This isn't your run-of-the-mill kind of hostage situation. Besides, we have these." He nodded back at the gun rack where three rifles resided. "But we likely won't need them. Jay Begay gets drunk a lot, sometimes does crazy things. We got a call he was waving a rifle about, threatening to shoot someone in the house if people got too close. We don't know who's in there. He's got a wife and a seventeen-year-old daughter." Jimmy shrugged. "Could be something, could be nothing."

"What's the plan?"

Jimmy paused to slow the truck and turn south onto a rut-filled dirt road. Zack saw the dust from Eagle Feather's pickup on beyond.

"I will be chief negotiator," Jimmy said. "I know Jay. I've been called out here before."

"So why the heavy presence?"

"You just don't know. Every time is a little different." He shrugged. "But we'll see when we get there." He peered at Zack. "You will be the federal representative. Stay in the truck, don't come out unless I indicate you should."

Zack nodded toward Eagle Feather's truck up ahead. "What will they do?"

"Eagle Feather and Lané will try to get within rifle range or closer unseen. They are backup in case things go wrong."

Zack glanced at Jimmy. "Like if he shoots you from the house?"

Jimmy grinned, shook his head. "Won't come to that."

Their road followed the swells and dips of the land, down into arroyos and steeply up the far sides. It kept them pointed toward a rock formation of several spires united by a common pedestal. As they neared, Zack saw a building at the base of the sandstone outcrop. It looked like a toy against the massive stone fin.

The road leveled and ploughed on, a red earth slash through the sage and cacti. Zack realized the dust from Eagle Feather's truck was no longer up ahead. "What happened to them?"

"We're close now," Jimmy said. "Eagle Feather won't let dust give away his presence. He'll slow down to avoid it." He looked at his watch, slowed their speed. "We'll take our time now, let them get set."

"And stop raising dust?"

Jimmy glanced at him. "We want to raise dust. We are the decoy."

"Oh." Zack began to grasp what was happening. So far, this was all quite different from what he'd been taught to expect.

THE DARK ROAD

The rock formation that was the backdrop for Jay Begay's dwelling grew to its true proportions as they neared, a shear wall of sandstone reaching several hundred feet toward the sky and a mile wide. Begay evidently utilized the wall as one section of fence, the rest a combination of barbed wire, stones and even a few large tires. A shed, a three-sided lean-to opened to the enclosure at a point close to a hogan with a pickup truck next to it. Another hogan stood one hundred yards away.

"Do two families live here?" Zack asked.

Jimmy shook his head. "Jay's family keeps a winter hogan and a summer hogan, but mostly live in the winter hogan, which is more substantial. He'll be in there, likely."

When the Bronco came within one hundred yards of the residence, Jimmy stopped and turned off the ignition. They sat still. Zack glanced at him.

Jimmy answered his look. "It is a courtesy to wait to be recognized when approaching someone's home." He raised his brows. "Especially at a time like this."

It was several long minutes before the door of the hogan opened and a figure stepped out, a woman dressed in a long skirt with a concha belt and a necklace dangling over a black jacket. She stood, arms crossed, and stared at them.

"Is this good or bad?"

"Hard to tell," Jimmy said. "That's Jay's wife, Emma. She runs the place until he gets really pickled." He stared. "She's not waving us on in, so something's up." His hand went to the door handle, he looked at Zack. "After I get out, take down the Winchester and keep it ready." He pushed open the door and stepped out and moved to the open.

Zack reached behind him and lifted the rifle from the top of the rack. He checked the load and held the weapon between his knees in the narrow confines of the cab. He watched Jimmy raise both arms to show he was unarmed.

"Yá'át'ééh. I see you, Emma. Are you well?"

Emma did not move, but her voice was strong and calm. She responded in Navajo.

"She says she is well and asks about me," Jimmy said, keeping his eyes on her. He replied in Navajo.

She spoke again.

"She says Jay wishes to know who the white man is in my truck," Jimmy said, then replied in her language. "I told her you are an FBI agent here to see no federal laws are broken."

The woman spoke again. Jimmy replied. Emma then turned and reentered the house.

Jimmy stood where he was, but turned to look toward Zack. "This is the tricky moment. I told her holding another person against their will is contrary to federal law. I asked to see Zenia, his daughter."

They waited. The sun through the windshield heated the truck interior like an oven. Zack's shirt wilted even more and stuck to his body while sweat trickled down to his waist. He wiped the sweaty hand holding the rifle on his pants.

The hogan door flung open. A man emerged. He was dressed in leggings and shirtless. His hair was tied back with a headband. He held a rifle with both hands, the barrel pointing skyward. He spoke in a hoarse guttural voice.

Jimmy replied—calm, reassuring.

The man waved the rifle about with one hand as he spoke. His voice was angry, harsh.

While the man ranted, Jimmy translated for Zack. "He wants to know by what right any man intrudes into his private affairs. He is very drunk and very angry." The tirade continued. "He is working himself up to something. Be ready to toss me the rifle."

Zack wiped his damp hands again and re-gripped the Winchester.

The man's guttural harsh stream of anger grew even more. Without warning, he snapped the rifle up to his shoulder.

"Now," Jimmy yelled and stepped behind the open door of the Bronco.

Zack propelled the rifle toward him, barrel first. As he did, he heard the ping of a bullet as it struck something in the front of the truck. Jimmy had the rifle now, resting the barrel on the hinge between door and truck body. It was aimed at Jay, but he did not fire. Zack saw why.

Two men, Eagle Feather and the Navajo policeman Lané were there having materialized on either side of the drunk Navajo with rifles pointed at him. Jay Begay lowered his rifle barrel, then dropped the weapon to the ground.

Jimmy handed the Winchester back to Zack, who replaced it in the rack and climbed out of the truck. He was sweating profusely now. He felt the welcome breeze over his damp body and wondered if he could possibly get any wetter. He followed Jimmy toward the hogan where the erstwhile shooter was now on his knees with arms cuffed behind him.

Zack heard the Navajos conversing as old friends as he neared, as if a bullet had never been fired with intent to harm. Emma and another woman emerged from the house, the second woman an attractive young girl dressed in jeans and a blouse. The

13

women stared at Zack, apparently less concerned by the life-threatening situation that just ended than curious at the appearance of a stranger in their midst. Then, as if choreographed, all the Navajos, prisoner included, stared at Zack and burst into laughter.

Zack was shocked and confused. Emma, the older woman, held her hand to her mouth and giggled. Jimmy and Lané grinned broadly. It was Eagle Feather who finally explained.

"You look like a burrito left out in a rainstorm, White Man."

Zack looked down at his shirt, wet, streaked with dirt, plastered against his white skin now red in places from heat rash, the tie flapped over his shoulder, pants wringing wet and pressed against skin, black polished shoes grimy with red dust. He could feel the too-large reservation hat slipping over his ears, his face was flushed and wet with sweat. He was a mess.

He looked at the amused faces of lawmen, prisoner, and family. Then he shrugged and broke into a broad grin. He did not know it at the time, but his acceptance on the Reservation began at that moment.

CHAPTER THREE

Mercifully, Jimmy received a radio request to drive Zack directly to the Quality Inn Navajo Nation in Tuba City where a room was set aside for him. Lané and Eagle Feather would bring the prisoner to Elk Wells where he would occupy a jail cell until a plan for his future was made. The case of Jay Begay was left to the Navajo Nation Police while the FBI moved on to more important matters.

Zack's suitcase was transferred to the Bronco and was in hand when Zack checked in at the motel desk. With studied non-response to Zack's appearance the young woman handed him a key and directed him to a room, a double bed suite. The small space would serve as home and office until he could find other living arrangements. Zack could not be happier.

After a long soaking shower, he put on clean, dry clothes and went to the Hogan Restaurant for a large burger. For the first time since his arrival in Arizona, he felt in command of himself. His training would begin tomorrow, but for now, his time was his own. His meal, whether late lunch or early dinner—his stomach would tell him later—was leisurely and pleasant, the food excellent. As he paid his bill the host suggested he visit the Explore Navajo Museum next door.

Ever diligent, Zack had begun researching the Navajo people as soon as he had learned his assignment, but there had been little time. The host assured him he would learn plenty at the museum. He was right. Zack spent several hours in the building, enough to realize he had barely scratched the surface. On his way out, he stopped at the paperback book rack and purchased several novels related to the Navajo. He'd continue his research that evening in a more relaxed way.

It was twilight when he returned to the motel. The air had cooled, the smell of lavender engulfed the entranceway. It had a calming effect. He envisioned himself slipping between cool sheets with his new book, and then—sleep.

It was not to be.

The lanky figure of Jimmy Chaparral rose from the lobby couch as Zack entered. The Navajo policeman grinned, a little apologetically. "You up for a night patrol?"

Zack was momentarily at a loss for words. The simple answer was no, but he suspected that response was not an option. He quickly learned he was right.

"Not my idea," Jimmy said, palms in the air. "Your boss asked me to take you out on this call. He wants you to experience some of what we do here. He doesn't think the academy trained you for some of this."

Zack found his second wind somehow. "Let me grab boots and a jacket."

Jimmy nodded. "I'll be right here."

This time Zack slipped on his shoulder holster and pistol. He reappeared downstairs in sturdy hiking boots and a light jacket. "I'm ready."

The Bronco was parked behind the building. Jimmy led the way down the corridor past the first floor rooms and out the back exit. Zack slipped into the now familiar passenger seat.

"What's up?" he asked, securing his belt tightly against the anticipated bounces and swerves of the vehicle.

"Animal mutilations," Jimmy said. He glanced at Zack and grinned.

Zack was startled. "No offense, but you say my boss wants me to come with you to see animal mutilations?"

"That's about the size of it." Jimmy shrugged, went on. "It's a common complaint out here. When you live close to nature, miles from anywhere, your resources are minimal. A man has fifty sheep, which are his livelihood. One night something kills one of them." Jimmy flicked a glance at Zack. "Could be a predator, a coyote, bear, whatever. It happens. But"—Jimmy paused while he negotiated the turn east onto Route 160—"lately there have been purposeless animal killings, as if simply for pleasure rather than food. These kills can happen night after night. It doesn't take long for the farmer to go out of business."

"What's causing it?"

Jimmy shrugged. "Don't know. But the farmer will tell you it's skinwalkers, or witches, or ghosts."

Zack laughed.

Jimmy looked full at him, not smiling. "I suspect that is why your boss wanted you to go with me."

Confused, Zack had no answer.

They rode in silence. It was dusk, the sun nearly gone, trees and fences along the way blurred, distant objects were shrouded and formless.

"What's tonight's situation?" Zack asked after a while.

"I don't know. A man named Ashkii Nez called it in. He lives out beyond Shonto on a small ranch not far from the Shonto Trading Post. You'll see, it's pretty desolate out there."

"Is it his sheep?"

Jimmy nodded. "Lenana took the call. She said he'd already lost several sheep over the last few nights, didn't want to lose any more."

Zack glanced out the window at the blackness invading the land. "How far is this place?"

Jimmy grinned. "Not far. Another forty miles, maybe."

Zack had other questions. Why the urgency for mutilated sheep? Wouldn't it be too dark to inspect the scene? Wouldn't it be better to wait for the light of day? The sheep weren't going anywhere, were they? But he was new to the land and the people—and to the man seated next to him. He'd already been gently chastised, so he decided to hold his questions and wait and see.

A half hour later Jimmy slowed and turned left at the intersection with Route 98, then accelerated, leaving the lights of a filling station and marketplace diminishing behind them. They crossed out of the flatness of the valley, rising into rough upland. Darkness enveloped everything, not a twinkle of a light was visible anywhere. For Zack, it was like flying in a plane at night, nothing but blackness out the window, just the tremble and roar of the jet engines to convince him anything was happening at all. He didn't like that, either. Conversation in the cab was replaced by the radio, country music punctuated occasionally by a Navajo disk jockey. Despite the sudden jolts and sways of the Bronco, Zack drifted in and out of sleep. The long, strange day was taking its toll.

A hard turn and the stiff Bronco springs bouncing onto unimproved road awakened him abruptly. He had the sensation they were ascending. He glanced at Jimmy, who saw he was awake.

"We're making a short side trip to the old Shonto Trading Post," he said. "It sits up on top of this plateau. Ashkii lives in a narrow valley down on the other side, just another fifteen minutes."

The air outside had cooled quickly with the setting of the sun. Zack was aware of the smell of mesquite and the occasional pungent aroma of pine.

"There's the old trading post. A neighbor called worried about kids sneaking in there at night."

Zack searched into the blackness and saw a tiny glow of light.

Jimmy turned off the radio. "Funny to see a light. The trading post is supposedly closed." He turned off the Bronco headlights and killed the engine. They listened. Zack's eyes adjusted and he could see the vague outline of a low, trailer-like building. As they watched, the light went out.

Jimmy opened his door and put a foot on the ground, standing part in and part out of the vehicle as he studied the building.

"What do you think?" Zack asked.

It was a moment before Jimmy replied. "Someone knows we're here but doesn't want us to know about him."

Zack heard the rustle of branches from the night breeze, the chirping of an insect somewhere. He became aware of the moonlight gently bathing the scene. The smell of earth and dry vegetation came to his nostrils, but there was something else.

"Someone has been smoking," he said. A slave to tobacco in his early years, Zack's nose had developed a hyper awareness of the smell.

Jimmy sent a glance his way. "More than one, I think." He stood listening, waiting.

"Is no one supposed to be here?"

Jimmy gave a shrug. "It's not so much that, it's their furtiveness." He shrugged again, climbed back into the Bronco.

"Probably just a bunch of kids, like they said." He started the engine. "We've got a long enough night as it is without adding to it." He backed into a turn and drove away from the trading post. "I'll file it in my report," he said as an afterthought. "Someone will catch them sooner or later."

A few minutes later, Zack sensed they were driving steeply downward. They were apparently on the shadow side of the ridge from the moon for it was as dark out there as he'd ever known, and the Bronco headlights with their coating of dust did little to help. Jimmy, however, seemed completely familiar with the road.

The vehicle bucked and bounced, once or twice thumping so hard the entire floor vibrated. They were in a macabre world where roadside vegetation came pale in the headlights and turned black as they passed.

Zack's anxiety was heightened when Jimmy turned the headlights off completely. They drove a short distance blind. Then Jimmy stopped the vehicle, killed the engine and set the brake.

"We are here," he said quietly.

"Here where?" Zack saw nothing but blackness.

Jimmy gave a low chuckle. "We are where we can observe the mutilated sheep. Twenty feet that way is the cliff edge. Directly beneath is the pasture where Ashkii keeps his sheep. His hogan is a half mile east of here." Jimmy busied himself rummaging in the back seat as he spoke. "Whoever is mutilating those sheep has come every night for three nights, according to him. There is a good chance he will come again tonight." He passed a heavy cylindrical object to Zack, a flashlight. "Do not turn it on under any circumstances unless I tell you." He pushed something else at Zack. "Your pistol will do little good from up here. Take this rifle. It's a Winchester Model 700 Police Rifle with a night scope and a ten-round magazine. Have you shot one before?"

Zack hefted the rifle. It felt barrel heavy. "No, I've only seen them in use."

"It's a free floating barrel, a bit heavy, but very accurate. Aim it just as you would any sniper rifle. Hopefully, we won't need to fire at all." He touched Zack's shoulder. "When we leave the vehicle, make no sound, move slow and easy. We have all night." Jimmy chuckled again. "Just follow me."

The first loud noise was the creak of the Bronco door as Zack opened it. Already he'd managed to fail his instructions, he thought. He closed the door inch by inch, didn't let it latch, and followed the vague form of the Navajo policeman. They crept through creosote and mesquite, holding branches against back swipe, footfalls muffled by sand. When Jimmy stopped and his form lowered, Zack came beside him and crouched.

Jimmy touched him, whispered, "The cliff is just in front of you. The small light below is Ashkii Nez's hogan. The sheep are a third of the way between us and his light. Can you see them?"

Zack stared down into a world of shadows. Was the man serious? Who could see anything?

"Don't worry, if you need to shoot, you'll know where to aim." A pat on the shoulder. "Get comfortable."

Zack searched until he found a rock large enough to support the rifle barrel and settled down behind it, moving several sharp objects out of the way. He waited with no idea what to expect. A night creature gave voice, a bird-like sound. A whisper of breeze stirred branches in a pinyon nearby. The night was cool, not at all unpleasant, the smell of the sage near him strangely comforting. Even his vision improved as time went on. The moon

21

was not yet visible behind them but shed more light and for the first time Zack saw the edge of the precipice in front of him. Some objects below took shape, a line of fence posts, some kind of vegetation. He didn't see any sheep.

Zack fought sleep. An early start to the day, his long flight, the hot wait at the airport, the tense confrontation with the rifle-bearing drunk, the long drive out here, the strangeness of it all, and now the pleasant coolness of the night all conspired to bring his eyelids creeping down. He dozed.

A staccato explosion near his ear startled and confused him. He let the flashlight fall to the ground and gripped the rifle with both hands as his awakening brain struggled to grasp what was happening.

CHAPTER FOUR

"Got 'em!" Jimmy's triumphant exclamation rushed Zack's brain back to reality. He remembered now. He was at a cliff edge overlooking a sheep flock somewhere near a trading post on the Navajo Nation Reservation, holding a rifle. Evidently, Sergeant Chaparral had just fired his weapon.

"Got what?"

Jimmy stood at the cliff edge, his flashlight beaming down on some indistinct creature thrashing about. As the men watched, the movement stopped.

"A coyote, I think," Jimmy said. "I figured it would be something like that."

Zack located his flashlight and added its beam to Jimmy's, creating a slightly brighter spotlight on two creatures, one dark and the other white, presumably a sheep. Neither moved. "What else would it be?"

"Well, there are other possibilities, but I'm glad we don't have to go into it."

Jimmy turned back from the cliff edge, favoring a knee as he walked. "My knees sure get stiff crouching like that." He turned to glance at Zack. "Have a nice snooze?"

Zack was embarrassed. He had hoped his involuntary time out had gone unnoticed.

"No problem," Jimmy said. "Just teasing. Totally expected, after a day like you've had."

Zack did not reply. He was not as ready to forgive himself.

They climbed into the Bronco, no longer hampered by a need for stealth. Jimmy started it up, put on headlights and steered off the embankment back onto the road. They endured several more bottoming ruts on the steep descent until they dropped into a level wash. Here the road was constructed of the alluvium and sand that filled the wash and was much smoother. The surrounding bluffs faded away into darkness and they were in open country.

Jimmy slowed, turned off the gravel course and stopped the vehicle near a fence held loosely together by barbed wire. "Shanks Mare and flashlights from here," he said.

Zack creaked open his door. "Rifles?"

"Suit yourself. Shouldn't need 'em, though."

Zack thought about it. His Glock 19M 9mm service revolver rode comfortably in his holster. The creature was dead. He shouldn't need the rifle.

Jimmy brought his, though. Zack held it for him and handed it back once the Navajo had negotiated the fence. Jimmy put a boot on a lower wire to allow Zack to slither through, although not without a tug and a rip. Jimmy cast about with his flashlight, decided on a direction and started off.

Zack followed.

The clouds had scuttled away for the moment, the moon edged brighter. Tall clumps of prickly pear appeared as dark upright figures, seeming to take on human characteristics. Several times Zack pulled up abruptly, startled until he was able to identify the objects for what they were.

Jimmy stopped, his beam searched. Zack came up beside him. The freshly mutilated body of a sheep lay on its back at his feet. Zack could now see the difference between butchered and mutilated. The sheep had been disfigured in ugly ways, as if the perpetrator were trying to obliterate its identity. The eyes were cut out, the tongue half missing and the genitals were gone along with partial disembowelment.

Zack stared, holding back an impulse to be sick. "A coyote did this?" he asked.

"Seems strange," Jimmy said. He shone his flashlight in a wider circle, hunting.

"What did you shoot?"

"That's what I'm starting to wonder." The Navajo began to walk in widening circles around the sheep's body, searching the ground.

Zack stared at the sheep's body. "Whatever did this inflicted great pain. It looks like an act of deliberate cruelty." He moved away from the sheep and helped with the search. When he heard Jimmy mutter under his breath, he moved closer and saw glistening blood on the dusty ground and a fur mound. It was a large coyote. It was dead, shot through the body. Jimmy knelt, brought his light close. After a moment he dug with his fingers in the soft soil beneath the animal and came up with a small object in his palm. He showed it to Zack.

"This is the slug from my rifle. This is the coyote I shot." He looked up at Zack. "This animal didn't kill that sheep, though. See, its tracks come from over there. It smelled the blood and was approaching the sheep when I shot it."

"So the sheep was already dead," Zack said. "Something else killed it. Can you track it?"

"Maybe." Jimmy walked back to the mutilated sheep, shone the flashlight around, then steadied it. "Just sheep prints," he muttered. The light beam searched, steadied, moved about. "There's something else here, but the sheep have obscured it." After fifteen minutes more of searching, Jimmy admitted defeat.

25

"That's it. I can't do any more until daylight." He looked at his watch. "It's too late to drive all the way back to Tuba City and return by dawn. We'll need to stay here tonight."

"Where?" Zack asked.

"We'll stay with Ashkii in his hogan. He lives alone and will not mind."

"What about my job, my boss?"

"Don't worry, I'll take care of all that."

Zack followed Jimmy back to the Bronco, his tired brain full of concerns. He had no fresh clothes, no personal items. He was about to spend the night with two Navajo men in the home of a complete stranger. He knew little about the customs of these people. How many social offenses might he commit without even knowing it? Then there was the matter of his new position. Would Agent Ben Brewster really understand when Zack wasn't ready to begin work tomorrow morning?

Another thought crossed his tired mind. When Jimmy swept him away from the motel for this adventure, Zack had taken the Navajo's word. He'd simply followed the man out the door. What if he hadn't said anything to Brewster at all? Maybe he simply grabbed the opportunity to get Zack's help in a purely Navajo matter.

Zack's final thought in his argument with himself was to stop thinking. He was too tired to make sense. Whatever his situation next morning, that would be the time to deal with it. Not now.

It took only minutes to drive to Ashkii's hogan. The moon was bright when Zack stepped out of the Bronco, the clouds had vanished. Zack glanced back in the direction they'd come. Moonlight bathed the ground and gilded the scrub, long shadows of fence posts marched off in a line toward the darkness of the cliff wall. Looking up at the heights he saw black silhouettes of pinyon pine and rock outcrops where the moon presented a bright backdrop...and there was something else—a figure, tall like a human, black, unmoving. Startled, Zack stared.

He turned to point it out to Jimmy, but the Navajo had disappeared around the side of the hogan. When Zack turned back, the figure was gone.

Zack hurried along the gravel path to the east side of the hogan where Jimmy was at the open door speaking in Navajo to another man. They brought Zack inside and introductions were made. Jimmy and Ashkii seemed to enjoy the moment to catch up and as the two spoke in Navajo, Zack looked around. The inside of Ashkii's hogan was not at all what he expected. He didn't really know what to expect, but he was surprised by how vibrant it was. Coming from darkness to the hogan interior bursting with color was like a watching a rose emerge from its bud. The walls were festooned with brightly decorated rugs and hangings of all sizes. Several watercolor landscape prints of pink mesas adorned the empty spaces between the hangings.

The interior space seemed larger than the outside suggested. Perhaps it was the simplicity of the furniture, the way it was arranged to give a look of openness or perhaps the height of the ceiling. The floor was hard packed earth with rugs scattered about, a tarp here, some sheepskins there. A floor to ceiling panel separated a small area, presumably Ashkii's bedroom. Zack caught a glimpse of a bed with a red and blue blanket. In the very center of the hogan was a simple stove with a stovepipe up through the ceiling. In contrast at the west wall there was a modern fireplace with a simple but elegant wooden mantle which held a framed photo of a family moment; a man, wife, little boy. Beneath it burned a cheery fire. It all felt extraordinarily comfortable to Zack. From the moment he had entered the building he'd felt warm and safe.

Ashkii himself was shorter than Zack by a foot, with a broad face and was of a stocky build. The leathery creases around his mouth and eyes gave him a good natured appearance. He beckoned Zack to a comfortable looking hammock chair and pressed a hot cup of tea into his hand.

Ashkii turned back to the stove.

"We will be having mutton stew soon," Jimmy said to Zack with a smile. "That's what smells so good."

"I'm really not so hungry."

"You can manage to eat. Navajo hospitality demands Ashkii feed his guests. Courtesy demands we at least pretend to enjoy it. Fact is, I think you'll be glad you did."

And he was. The stew was wonderful, an intricate mixture of meat, vegetables and spices that drove hunger before it like dogs drive sheep. Zack ate more than he thought possible. While they ate, seated cross-legged on the floor, Jimmy chatted with Ashkii who spoke English well.

"I killed the coyote, but it had not harmed your sheep."

"But one was dead."

"Mangled beyond belief," Jimmy said with a sidelong look at Zack.

"Could you see what killed it?"

"No. I searched for prints or signs, but it was too dark."

"There, you see," Ashkii said, his shoulders settling as if the issue was resolved.

"I will know better in the morning light," Jimmy said.

28

Zack finished his stew and set aside the bowl. The warmth of the room and a full tummy conspired together, and his eyelids drooped.

Ashkii noticed. He rolled out two straw mats near the stove and set blankets and pillows on them. Zack gratefully went there, pulled the blanket over himself and fell asleep. At some point, he surfaced just long enough to hear low conversation and smell tobacco smoke before he plunged back into blackness.

CHAPTER FIVE

An unfamiliar sound drew Zack to consciousness from confused sleep. Beyond his closed eyelids he was aware of light imbued with that peculiar quality of sunrise. There was a silence to this dawn; no roar of busses or accelerating cars spiked with jabby horns, no distant sirens. Just the soft chanting that had awakened him.

He opened his eyes and allowed them to wander without raising his head, bringing to memory the straw pallet, the coarse but warm blanket. His eyes followed the packed dirt floor to a shadow and to the back of the legs of a man standing at the doorway, old calves with blue veins across still well defined musculature, that of an active walker.

Ashkii was facing the sun, swaying slightly as he sang a soft three or four pitch song. Zack did not know what words the Navajo was singing, but remembered mention of greeting the dawn at the Navajo Museum.

The chanting ceased. Zack watched the calves tense and move as the man turned. Zack lifted his head. Ashkii's smile reminded him of his grandfather.

"I have greeted the day," he said. "There is a good chill to the air. I will prepare food now. Jimmy will be back soon. If you need to pee, the outhouse is behind the hogan. You can wash at the pump." Ashkii shuffled off behind the divider.

Zack sat up and stretched. As his covers fell away, he felt the cold air stream in from the open doorway. He quickly folded the blanket and rolled the mat, securing it with the attached thongs, and left the bedding in a neat stack by the stove. He stepped outside, blinking at the bright sun and walked to the rear of the hogan. There he found the crude shed-like outhouse. At the pump, it took several strong thrusts to release the flow and the water was cold. By now Zack was completely awake. He launched into a series of exercises from his training. After the last jumping jack, he saw Jimmy watching him and smiling.

"Typical white man, always stirring up dust."

Zack grinned. "Sorry."

He followed Jimmy back into the hogan. Where Zack's bedding had been, Ashkii now knelt, encouraging flame to life inside the stove. Jimmy went to sit cross-legged on a faded blanket near the hogan wall. Zack followed his example.

Without looking away from his task, Ashkii began to speak softly in Navajo. Jimmy replied. After a lengthy discussion he turned to Zack.

"We were talking about my look around this morning. I have told Ashkii whatever killed the sheep did not return last night. The dead coyote is where we left it."

"Did you find anything else this morning?" Zack asked.

"No more than we saw last night."

Ashkii turned from the stove where tortillas were browning in a pan and looked at Zack. "Jimmy does not believe the sheep are being killed by an an'n ti' practicing his rites."

Jimmy shrugged, looked at Zack. "He means a witch."

"Why would he think that?"

Ashkii was busy with his food preparations and seemed oblivious to the two men.

Jimmy sighed. "He has much to support this thought, from the Navajo view. The sheep was not killed for food. It is hard to explain why it was mutilated the way it was. I found no signs from the killer, whatever it was; not last night, not this morning."

"But you don't believe it was something supernatural, do you?"

Jimmy chuckled. "Ben was pleased to hear about it. This is the kind of thing he hoped you would see."

Zack looked at him with eyebrows raised. "You spoke to Agent Brewster?"

Jimmy nodded. "I called him on the SAT phone this morning to explain. He said I may keep you to finish up."

Ashkii muttered, "You will take the belagaana to find a witch."

"It is more likely I will take Agent Tolliver to watch me file this case as unsolved."

Just then Zack recalled the strange figure. "I almost forgot. There was someone up on the cliff top last night looking down at us."

Both men turned and looked at him.

"When? Where?" Jimmy asked.

"It was just after we arrived here. I looked up when we climbed out of the car and saw this man-like figure against the moon. I turned to show you, but you had already gone. By the time I looked back, it wasn't there."

"What did it look like?"

"I couldn't tell. It was just a dark silhouette. I can't even say for sure it was human, except it was standing upright like one."

Jimmy gave Zack a long look. "Well, that at least gives us something to investigate. We'll stop and take a look on our way back." He turned at Ashkii. "I'll ask Eagle Feather to come out here to have a look at your sheep."

Ashkii nodded.

After a tasty, filling breakfast, Zack and Jimmy took their leave of Ashkii. For Zack, the overnight had been an eye opening experience and would be a special memory.

The interior of the Bronco was already hot when they climbed in. On the way back up the grade, Zack asked, "Why would you send Eagle Feather all the way out here to do what you have already done?"

Jimmy shot a glance at Zack. "Eagle Feather is the best tracker in the world."

Zack was surprised. "Well, that covers a lot of territory."

"I have never seen his equal. Nor has anyone I know who has hunted with him. It is why he makes such a good living as a guide. His reputation is worldwide."

Zack was intrigued. "If he does so well, why does he drive that battered up old truck?"

Jimmy chuckled. "Yes, and why does he live in a little tin trailer on an isolated mesa? For that matter, why does he lend his skills to the Navajo Police but never accept payment? We have all wondered about that." He grinned. "But his money is soon gone, I am told."

"What is his vice? Gambling? Drinking?"

"Charity, actually. Almost as soon as he is paid, some Navajo child receives a big clothing allowance or a Navajo student receives a year of college for free." He chuckled. "And Eagle Feather is still seen crawling under the hood of that old pickup trying to fix something with bailing wire."

"No wife, family?"

"Nope."

Jimmy steered the Bronco off the road and set the brake. "Here we are. This is where I shot the coyote last night. Let's take a look around."

Despite the training he'd received at the Academy, Zack knew he was watching a far superior tracker. He saw where Jimmy's eyes went, what he touched and didn't touch as the Navajo worked close to the cliff edge. His "look around," as he called it, took twenty minutes. As they walked back to the truck Jimmy said, "I found no sign of anyone there but you and me."

Zack's confidence ebbed. "I guess I could have been mistaken. I was very tired, the moonlight and shadows did strange things, I—"

"I think you saw exactly what you thought you saw. I found no sign someone was there, but I could sense it."

The men rode in silence. Zack pondered what Jimmy had just said. He learned in training an FBI agent should never act upon a feeling and certainly not commit resources based upon something less than solid evidence. He wondered what Jimmy would do.

They stopped at the Shonto Trading Post. It looked very different in the daylight. Jagged sandstone cliffs towered behind it decorated with green bits of clinging pinyon. The building itself was whitewashed adobe. A white clapboard building with sloped-roof stood at right angles with Historic Shonto Trading Post, Navajo Rugs-Baskets-Pottery written on the side along with a picture of a traditional Navajo rug. Under a short porch with wooden posts a sturdy looking door at the entranceway was padlocked.

"I'm going to take a look around here," Jimmy said.

Jimmy started toward the rear of the trading post. Zack ambled over to the front of the deserted store. He read some out of date notices. Advertisements for products long gone were painted over with whitewash. By the time he had worked his way along the front of the building, Jimmy was back.

They drove away. Jimmy said nothing for a while. He seemed to be thinking about something.

"Someone broke into the trading post last night," he said at last.

"What now?"

"I called the owners. All their inventory is relocated, their only concern is its possible use as a drug habitat."

"What will they do?"

"I expect they'll put better locks on the doors. It's a historic building, they don't want it trashed."

Zack nodded.

Jimmy grinned. "I was right about kids. They were around there smoking something last night. But they weren't the ones broke in. There was someone else around." He glanced at Zack. "Maybe the same guy you saw at the top of the cliff last night."

CHAPTER SIX

The aroma of coffee rising to his nostrils felt nearly as wonderful as drinking it. Zack was at a table in a small cafe in Elk Wells, with a hovering mothering waitress nearby ready to meet all his needs. The coffee was great, but it wouldn't have mattered so long as it had caffeine.

"Are you Kate, the owner?" Zack asked. The name of the restaurant was Kate's Cafe.

She smiled shyly and nodded while continuing to wipe tables that already glistened. Zack was her lone customer at the moment. He figured it was because he was late for breakfast but early for lunch. He and Jimmy had arrived late last night after an afternoon interviewing residents of homes in the vicinity of the trading post. After that, Zack flopped in one of two unoccupied jail cells for the night. The bed was comfortable, the cell spotlessly clean—he'd experienced less desirable motel rooms. He'd have slept well in any event, as tired as he was.

He woke late this morning. Apparently, the policemen had been in and out pursuing their normal duties and he'd not even twitched. Jimmy was gone when he awoke, but the woman named Lenana had pointed to the shower and later written out a chit for free breakfast at Kate's. Zack was starting to get used to putting on the same old underwear; it looked like he was going to save money on laundry bills in this job.

A bell jingled and Kate walked over to the chef's window and picked up a steaming plate. She brought it over and set it down in front of Zack. On it were the inevitable tortillas, shredded lettuce, heaps of scrambled egg, sausage, and a biscuit. Zack was almost overcome by the delicious smells.

"Can I get you anything else?" Her voice was low and gentle.

Zack shook his head, his eyes glued to the piled up plate before him.

"There's ketchup there, and butter and syrup. We can get you hot sauce if you like, or mayo?"

"Why don't you just let the poor man eat his food?" Jimmy's voice came from the door where he'd just entered. Zack waved him over.

Kate gave Zack a final smile and bustled away.

Jimmy came and pulled out a chair. "Go ahead, eat, don't mind me." He signaled Kate for coffee.

Zack rolled some egg and lettuce in a tortilla and took a large bite. He chewed, swallowed, looked at Jimmy. "You were out early."

"Yeah. Five this morning to be exact. Got a call about a man dead just off the road out near Shonto."

Zack's eyebrows rose. "Is this normal? I mean a body before breakfast?"

Jimmy shook his head. "No. Usually two or three." He grinned as Zack stared. "This one is special, though. They found the dead man right near the place I shot the coyote that night."

"But we searched along there the next morning."

"Apparently, we searched the wrong side of the road. They found the body on the other side." He glanced at Zack. "C'mon, eat. We got work to do and you may not get another chance."

Zack scooped up some sausage and chewed obediently.

Kate arrived with Jimmy's coffee. He picked up the cup and took a long sip. "Ah, that's good."

"Am I still assigned to help you?" Zack asked.

Jimmy shook his head. "Nope. You're assigned back to Ben. This was a murder, a man was shot. Makes it a federal case. Ben's up there now with Eagle Feather."

Zack made a soundless "Oh" with his mouth and took another bite as his mind worked over the situation.

"I'm going to take you up there after you finish and leave you off," Jimmy said.

Zack gulped down some coffee. "You're not staying?"

"I'm a suspect. I can't go near the case. If things go bad enough, I could be put on suspension."

Zack's fork hung in the air again. "But you didn't shoot at anyone on top of the cliff. You shot the coyote below it."

"They've only got my word for that," Jimmy said. "And yours, 'cause by the way you are a witness. Ben will want to interview you soon as you get out there."

By now the passenger seat in the Bronco was very familiar to Zack. It was another dry hot yet beautiful day in Arizona. He was gradually becoming accustomed to the size of the world around him which sometimes meant he could often see his destination from fifty miles away. Back East he traveled tree to tree.

The return route to the intersection with Route 98 was the same as the prior evening but looked entirely different in the morning light. The distant buttes cast long shadows and their rims shimmered as if on fire.

"Who was killed? Did you know him?" Zack asked.

Jimmy shook his head. "No. If they know who it is, they didn't tell me."

Zack digested that. "What will you be doing this morning?"

"Well, sir, now that the feds have Jay Begay in custody in Tuba City, I will check in on Emma and Zenia. After that, I'll report back to the office where Lenana will have a list of things to do as long as my arm."

"Don't you have any help?"

"Sure. You saw the officers there. We are a small force in a small town, but we patrol a large area." Jimmy swept a hand to encompass all the terrain around them. "Often it's not so much the number of incidents as it is the number of miles that take up our time."

Zack shook his head, trying to fathom it. In Virginia, six officers might respond to the same call.

The road turned to gravel beyond the trading post. With the windows open, all Zack's efforts to return to cleanliness in the jail shower came to naught. By the time they arrived at their destination there was grit in his teeth and the now familiar smell of dry dust in his nose.

Three vehicles were parked along the road. Zack recognized Eagle Feather's rust-red truck. A mobile crime scene vehicle was there, the large side panel of the truck open and someone in white coveralls busy. Across the narrow road a black Ford all-wheel-drive SUV was partially off the road on the cliff side. Yellow crime tape stretched between a couple of pinyon trees a short distance from the crime scene truck. Two men stood together talking, both in shirtsleeves.

"Here's your stop," Jimmy said.

As soon as Zack stepped out and shut the door Jimmy swung the Bronco into a K turn and roared back the way they had come.

Zack saw Ben standing by the yellow tape. He walked over to him.

Ben turned at his approach. "Good morning, Agent Tolliver. I see Sergeant Chaparral has kept you entertained."

"Yes, sir."

"This is Agent Scott Witherspoon from the Flagstaff office. He happened to be up this way, fortunately for us."

Witherspoon was a lanky man, tall with sandy hair, pale features and big hands, one of which he offered Zack. "Welcome to Arizona."

Zack shook the hand. "Thank you."

"We keeping you busy enough?" he asked.

"Sure enough."

Ben motioned. "You might have noticed we got a body over here, Agent Tolliver. Come take a look." He stepped over the tape.

Zack followed and walked a few steps to where a small pinyon partially obscured the body of a man, on his back, arms stretched to either side. His features and dark skin suggested he was Native American. The man was of stocky build, wore a flannel shirt and blue jeans with a thick leather belt. His boots were scuffed, the heals worn down.

"Does anyone know him?" Zack asked.

Ben shook his head. "None of us have seen him before, best we can remember. Sergeant Chaparral called me this morning soon as he learned about the murder, said he'd been right here with you yesterday. He's an experienced officer, knew he'd have to back off the case and he left it to Officer Shorter to contain and do preliminary work at the crime scene. He told me you'd seen a man standing at the cliff edge the night before, right over there. Can you tell us about it?"

Zack found himself staring at the body. This was the first dead man he'd seen before, let alone a murdered man at the scene of the crime. He expected to feel more than he did.

"We had been examining the mutilated sheep, trying to find some trace of the culprit, but no luck," he said. "The coyote Sergeant Chaparral killed hadn't yet reached the dead sheep, according to its tracks, so it couldn't have killed it. But we found no other tracks, no sign, nothing to show who or what mutilated it."

Agent Witherspoon said, "This man was shot in the abdomen. Takes a long time to die from that kind of a wound. After the initial impact and blood loss, he might've stemmed the flow and tried to get help somewhere. He might have made it this far."

It took Zack a while to grasp what the agent was saying. "You mean you think Jimmy shot this man, that the man then walked all the way up here to die? It's got to be a mile at least, and up a steep hill."

"It's not unheard of to get pretty far with a wound like that." The agent sounded a bit miffed for being doubted.

Ben's eyes flitted between the two men. "Agent Tolliver, you were about to tell me about the man you saw up on the cliff."

"I'm not positive it was a man, sir. After a thorough search for tracks around the dead sheep, we gave it up and went to spend the night with the sheep's owner, Ashkii Nez, figuring we'd look again in the daylight. So we drove to his hogan—"

41

"How far was that?" Ben asked.

"A quarter mile, maybe, no more. We were there in minutes. As soon as I stepped out of the Bronco I looked up toward the cliff. The moon was behind it, the figure was a shadow form just standing there apparently looking down at us."

"Did Sergeant Chaparral see it?" Witherspoon asked.

"No. As soon as I saw it, I turned to tell him but he'd already gone to the hogan. When I looked back, the figure was gone."

Ben studied Zack. "What's your best guess? Man or beast?"

"I...I don't know. It looked like a man, it seemed to be watching us. I mean, it was a long way away, in the dark." Zack sighed. "The figure was upright. If it was a bear, it was on two legs."

"What happened to Jimmy's rifle slug?" Ben asked.

"He gave it to Ashkii."

Ben glanced at Witherspoon. "We need to get down there and interview that shepherd." He turned to Zack. "Before all that, you were up here at the cliff edge, looking down at the sheep. What was the plan then?"

"We were setting up to watch the sheep. Apparently, the mutilations had occurred over several nights. Jimmy had a rifle, gave me one, and we were going to wait and see if anything bothered the sheep."

"How long did you wait?"

Zack felt embarrassed. "I'm not sure. I...uh, I might have dozed off. Jimmy's rifle shot startled me."

"Did you see what he was shooting at?"

Zack shook his head. "No."

"What happened then?"

"We shone our flashlights on something thrashing around near the sheep. It was hard to tell what it was, it was really too far to see clearly."

"Did Sergeant Chaparral say what he thought it was?" Witherspoon asked.

"Yeah, he said he thought it was a coyote."

Ben put a hand on Zack's shoulder. "The forensics team will be here a while longer. Agent Witherspoon and I are going down to interview the shepherd. Just keep an eye on things but keep out of everybody's way."

Zack watched the two agents work their way back to the road to the Ford SUV, climb in and start off in a spurt of dust. He saw there were two forensic specialists, one engaged in studying the ground around the body, the other occupied with something at the crime scene truck.

Zack thought about his responses to Ben's questions. Was there anything he missed? Was there anything else he should have done? Was it a mistake to confess to dozing off? Was he about to have a very short career?

Shrugging off those thoughts, he brought himself back to the present. He did not believe this dead man could have climbed all the way up here with a hole through his middle, then stand calmly at the cliff edge and peer down. He must have been killed up here. If so, he might have been lying there already dead even as he and Jimmy waited with their rifles at the cliff edge. If he'd been murdered after they drove away, would they have heard the shot? Maybe not, if they were in the Bronco.

Zack walked back to the road and crossed to the place where they had stood vigil the night before and peered over the edge. The sheep were almost directly below him, white mounds like so many rocks. Beyond was a line of fence, beyond that several sheds and buildings including Ashkii's hogan. It all seemed so close in the daylight. He guessed the sheep were no more than one hundred feet beneath him, maybe even less. But the cliff was sheer, a difficult climb even for a healthy man. The only other way to get here from down there was to walk over to the road. It was a very long walk for a man with a bullet hole in him. If he had been shot down there with the sheep, why not try to get to Ashkii's home instead? What would motivate the man to come up here?

Zack shook his head. It had to be coincidence. Jimmy shot a coyote and someone else shot this man. Was the murderer the figure he saw outlined by the moon? Zack gave an involuntary shudder as he realized the killer could have been lurking nearby the entire time he and Jimmy waited for the sheep attack.

"You do not believe Jimmy Chaparral shot this dead man." The words came from directly behind him, causing Zack to start. He knew even before he turned around it was Eagle Feather.

CHAPTER SEVEN

The Navajo regarded him with enigmatic eyes. He stood at ease, comfortable, the old Remington rifle tucked in his folded arms. The rim of his black hat rested just at his brows. He presented a tin-type figure of old time Navajo. Zack never heard him approach. How had the man gotten so close?

"You think someone else shot this man," Eagle Feather said. The eyes held him, pushed for a reply.

"I was thinking that, yes."

"You think the killer waited and after Jimmy made his shot and you drove away, he stood here and watched you examine the sheep and drive to Ashkii's hogan. It is true."

Zack was surprised. "How do you know that?"

Eagle Feather waved toward the cliff. "He showed me."

Zack automatically looked for prints at his feet, then realized the futility. "But Jimmy investigated here this morning."

"Jimmy is a good tracker." Eagle Feather's tone was ambiguous.

Zack let it go. "You think the murdered man was over there, already dead, while Jimmy and I waited here last night."

"Isn't that what you think?" Eagle Feather's eyes studied Zack's

Zack turned and looked into the valley. He saw the miniature dust cloud behind the car as it drove away from Ashkii's hogan. "Ben and Agent Witherspoon are returning," he said. "If they have Jimmy's rifle bullet they can test the blood traces and they will see he shot a coyote."

"They have the bullet?" Eagle Feather looked surprised.

"Yes, Jimmy gave it to Ashkii. He found it under the coyote."

Eagle Feather stared into the valley, then turned and walked away. Zack followed.

At the road, Eagle Feather paused. "You will tell the FBI men what we have said?"

"You are leaving?"

There was a glimmer in Eagle Feather's eye. "Very good. You keep getting better."

Several minutes after the dust settled behind Eagle Feather's truck the black SUV appeared from the other direction and pulled over near where Zack stood.

Ben leapt out. "Was that Eagle Feather?"

"Yes. He was just here," Zack said.

Ben stared at the dissipating dust. "He was supposed to report." He looked at Zack. "Did he tell you anything? Did he learn anything?"

Zack glanced from Ben to Agent Witherspoon. Both sets of eyes were on him. "Yes, I...we think someone else murdered the deceased. He...we think the man was already dead when Sergeant Chaparral and I arrived last night."

Witherspoon interrupted. "What's this I, we, he, me stuff!"

"Uh, just that I was thinking along the same lines—"

"So this idea just popped in your head, Agent?"

Ben made a brushing aside motion. "Let's get on with Eagle Feather's report, shall we?" He looked at Zack.

Zack nodded. "Eagle Feather believes the murderer was still here when we arrived and watched us from across the road someplace. After Sergeant Chaparral took his shot and we drove down to examine the results, the murderer came here and stood and watched us. That would be the man I saw standing above the cliff."

Ben studied Zack under furrowed brows. "He thinks the sheep mutilation and this murdered man have nothing to do with each other?"

Zack nodded. "Not directly, at least."

Witherspoon wore a look of impatience and disbelief. "One thing you'll learn in this job, agent, if you last long enough, is there usually is no such thing as coincidence." His voice was cold, dry, as if his soul lacked moisture. "Here's the way I see it. You and Sergeant Chaparral came here last night and he told you a cock 'n bull story about the sheep—to get himself a witness, see? He'd already arranged to meet the poor dead bugger over there. He knew you were tired from your trip, the culture shock, all that crap. He probably slipped something in your coffee, whatever. So you accommodate him, fall asleep, and he simply turns and shoots the guy waiting for him over there and turns back and shoots down into the valley as you wake up from the noise. When you see him, his rifle is aimed down and he's telling you he shot something down there. He knows a sheep has already been fucked up down there—maybe he did it himself—so he takes you there and shows you a dead coyote and—oh, yeah, he finds a slug in the ground—how lucky is that? And now, here comes the real genius: instead of taking you back to Tuba City where you might give things away to Ben here, he keeps you with him overnight and all the next day. Where? In a jail cell! That's rich. You sure can't talk to anybody from there, can you? Then when the body is finally discovered"—Witherspoon turned to Ben—"Who discovered it by the way? Did Chaparral give you a name?" His eyes came back to Zack. "That's when he drags you back out here to tell his story for him." A smug grin slathered Witherspoon's face.

Ben stared at Witherspoon. "Jesus!"

Zack was shocked. Where had all that come from? He never saw it coming. "But he shot a coyote. You have the bullet. You can match blood, DNA..."

Witherspoon grinned. He pulled a plastic bag from his pocket. "You mean this? Why bother? If it was planted, it'll just have coyote blood on it." He handed the bag to Ben.

Ben did not look pleased. "Listen, I've known Jimmy Chaparral a long time. He just wouldn't do something like this."

Witherspoon looked sympathetic. "Ben, you know as well as I do anybody can do anything given enough motivation. People do what they gotta do."

Ben yelled to the man at the crime scene truck. "Sig, can you come over here a minute?"

Sig looked up, nodded, and came over.

When he arrived, Ben said, "From your examination do you believe the victim was killed at the scene?"

Sig looked at the three agents. "It looks that way. He was shot from a distance in the center of the back, the bullet narrowly missing the spine and traveled directly through the abdomen and out the front. The exit wound is not large, suggesting minimal yawing of the bullet, thus likely from a high-powered rifle." He looked at Ben. "Hard to say, but I think he was alive when he arrived here and he died here; there may be enough blood to suggest that much."

"Enough blood to say he was shot here?"

"Again, hard to say. If the bullet came through relatively clean, there wouldn't necessarily be a lot of external bleeding."

Witherspoon leaned toward him. "Can you determine where the bullet came from given the body position, assuming he was shot and fell immediately?"

Sig thought about it. "My colleague might disagree. However, the man is lying on his back, arms spread, one knee raised. To my mind, he ran away from the road, was shot, stood where he was for a few moments, one knee buckled before the other, and he pivoted onto his back as he fell. If that scenario is true, the bullet would have come from the direction of the road."

A look of triumph flashed across Witherspoon's face.

Ben nodded to Sig. "Thank you. I have one more favor. Would you walk there and stand where you think the victim stood when he was shot, please?"

As Sig walked toward the yellow tape, Ben turned to Zack. "Agent Tolliver, please take us to the exact place Officer Chaparral was when you heard the shot."

Zack led the way back to the cliff edge. He recognized the boulder he had used to support his rifle. His eye traveled to the place Jimmy had been. "Right there," he said. He went and stood there.

Ben came and stood with him. He stared back across the road at Sig where he had positioned himself. There was undergrowth all around, but Sig stood clear. He waved, Ben waved back.

"It's a clear path to the victim," Ben said. He looked at Zack. "How dark was it?"

"It was quite dark. I had difficulty seeing anything down below, even with the big flashlight."

"But you had night scopes," Witherspoon said.

"Yes, we did."

Ben began a slow walk to the road, the others followed. Sig walked back to meet them near the black SUV.

Ben turned to Witherspoon. "The scenario you suggest is possible, although to my mind unlikely. There are a lot of loose ends. More likely, to my mind, is the murder had already been committed when Sergeant Chaparral and Agent Tolliver arrived here. The figure Tolliver saw might well have been the killer."

He turned to Sig, ticking off items on his finger. "We need to know definitively whether the man was killed here, or at least how far he could have walked with his wound. We need the hour of his death, as close as possible. We need a thorough search for the bullet that killed the victim. We need everything you can tell us from the wound." He handed the evidence bag to Sig. "I will collect the two rifles from Sergeant Chaparral for you to test. Oh, yeah, and have someone go down and look at those sheep remains and tell me what caused those mutilations."

"I might be able to help with that," Sig said. He extracted a large evidence bag from his white coat pocket. In it was a utility knife, the kind used to slice open boxes, with extractable blade. The blade was open, the whole knife covered in blood. "I found this in the brush near the victim," he said. "I'll test the blood for a source."

Witherspoon looked like the cat who ate the canary.

"I think that about covers it for now," Ben said.

Agent Witherspoon grinned. "I'd say it more than covers it."

Zack was adamant. "I only heard one shot. How could Sergeant Chaparral have shot a man in one direction and a coyote in the other with just one shot?"

Witherspoon shook his head sadly. "I'd have to say you are not the most credible witness, Agent Tolliver, since you admit to having fallen asleep."

Zack opened his mouth to argue.

Ben held up a hand. "I have to agree with Agent Witherspoon on that point." He opened the car door. "Nothing more we can do here. Agent Tolliver, climb in. Let's get you settled back at the office."

The ride back to Tuba City in the big air conditioned SUV was very different from the trips in Jimmy's Bronco. The suspension turned the roads into a lulling cradle and the powerful AC charged the space with renewed vigor. The two agents in the front seat spoke of other matters related to other cases they were working in tandem. Alone in the back seat, Zack went over his conversation with Eagle Feather in his mind. He wondered if Ben accepted Agent Witherspoon's theory for even a minute. He decided not to worry about it. The forensic evidence would undoubtedly expose its flaws.

When they reached Tuba City, at Zack's request, Ben dropped him off at the Quality Inn. Thirty minutes later, after a shower and change of clothes, Zack walked south along Main Street. Although his path took him right past the McDonalds and the noon sun was hot and he was very hungry, he didn't feel he could delay an appearance at the office for even a minute. Promising himself a burger at the first opportunity, he walked on.

The FBI Liaison Office was discreetly located near the Nanees 'Dizi, the local government office for the Navajo. The FBI office was a third party rental, very discreet. Zack pushed the shadowy glass entry door open and walked into a small waiting room facing a reception desk. A young woman with neatly coiffed black hair wearing a turquoise necklace and large silver bracelets on each wrist sat there. She raised her eyes at his appearance.

"May I help you?"

Zack noticed travel brochures on the desk's shiny metal surface, a pivoting rack of postcards nearby. Beyond the girl was a plain wood door secured with an electronic lock pad and glowing buttons. To his left was a wall adorned with travel posters. He could almost believe he was in the office of a travel agent.

He smiled at the girl. "I am Agent Zack Tolliver. I believe I am expected."

"May I see some identification, Agent Tolliver?" Her smile indicated she knew full well who he was.

Zack extracted his plasticized ID and handed it to her.

After a quick glance she handed it back and pressed a button. The locked door sprung open a few inches. "Go on in," she said. "Agent in Charge Brewster is expecting you, his office is the first door on your left." As he started that way she said, "Ignore the detector buzz; I'll get it programmed for you later."

Zack nodded and pushed through the door. A buzzer sounded as foretold, then was silenced. The first door on his left had a sign that read simply *Agent In Charge*. He knocked lightly.

There was a muffled "Come in!"

Zack stepped into Ben's office. He looked about in surprise. Every wall was lined with shelves, every shelf was loaded with books. Everything in the room, including the large desk before him, was made of rich walnut paneling. He felt as if he was in the inner sanctum of a library.

Ben watched his reaction from behind his desk and waved him toward a cushioned chair. "Have a seat. Let me just finish this report."

It took five minutes during which Zack let his eyes wander to the shelves. Immediately behind Ben were books of FBI protocol and procedures, forensic science, and weaponry. The other walls held books on Navajo culture, government, language, and history. Swinging his head the other way he found volumes on Native American prehistory, archaeology, ancient ruins of the American Southwest, native rock art and so on. A cough brought his head back around.

"I try to keep informed," Ben said.

"I need to spend months in here," Zack said, knowing it to be true.

"I doubt you'll have time for that. However, I do have one or two volumes I can recommend and will loan you to help you get up to speed with the folks you'll be assisting."

Zack nodded his appreciation.

Ben became all business. "But to the work at hand. Shortly I will ask Bella, my talented assistant, to show you to your office and set you up. But before that, we need to find an angle on this murder case and get it resolved. Time is of the essence. Generally, we don't need to worry about the Fourth Estate out here even in a murder case because in the eyes of Joe Public the natives are continually knocking each other off and thus murders on the Reservation are not news. But if a police officer is suspected of murder, even a Navajo police officer, the press will show interest."

Ben's eyes bored into Zack's. "Therefore, we must either exonerate Sergeant Chaparral or arrest him, pronto. When I say exonerate, I don't mean simply declaring he didn't do it—I mean finding the guy who did."

He wheeled his chair away from the desk and sat back. "Eagle Feather has not checked in. He's a bit...unpredictable, but you can't overstate his skills. He spoke to you. What exactly did he say?"

Zack shifted in his chair, crossed his legs. "Just what I told you out there. He thinks the murder victim was already dead when Jimmy and I arrived. Presumably the killer hid himself and saw Jimmy take his shot. Eagle Feather tracked a man to the spot where we had just been. The man had apparently gone there to watch us from the cliff top. I imagine he was curious to know what we were shooting at."

"And after that?"

Zack shrugged. "Eagle Feather didn't go beyond that."

"In fact, where did he go?"

"He didn't say."

"Okay. " Ben stared at his desk, deep in thought.

Zack waited.

Ben sighed. "Zack, I need a true answer. Could Jimmy have changed position enough to turn, search out his target, shoot, and turn back and shoot into the valley and you not realize it? Is that even possible?"

Zack thought, tried to remember. The sad truth was, he really must have dozed off. "I can't be certain, sir. I'd have to say it is just possible. I was very sleepy and have no memory of the time just before Jimmy's shot woke me."

"One shot."

"Yes, sir, I'm quite sure of that."

"Your gut?"

"I don't believe it."

Ben's desk phone rang. He picked it up, listened. "Thanks." He looked at Zack. "That was Lenana, Jimmy's assistant. She said Jimmy just got a missing person call up near Shonto.

CHAPTER EIGHT

Zack was on his way back to Elk Wells, this time driving the big black Ford. After Lenana's call, Ben had ordered him to go investigate the missing person incident. The dead man had not yet been identified. If he'd had a wallet or medicine bundle, it was now gone. Perhaps the missing person was the murder victim. Beyond that, Ben wanted Zack to keep an eye on Jimmy to see if he acted suspicious in any way.

A DNA check was in progress, also ballistic tests. Unfortunately, the slug that killed the mystery man had not been found. A needle in a haystack, as Sig had said, it could be anywhere. Ben assured Zack he'd contact him once any test results were made known.

When Zack pulled up in front of the police station in Elk Wells, Jimmy was already standing next to the Bronco. Zack lowered his window. "Want to ride in comfort?"

"Shush!" Jimmy said, nodding toward the Bronco. "You'll hurt the old girl's feelings." He pointed to a space. "Park that thing. Where we're going, we need good ground clearance."

Back in the Bronco, windows open, Zack felt the dust and sweat building up once again. The early afternoon sun was hot. "Where're we going?"

"Back up on the plateau. We're going to the town of Shonto."

"There's a town?"

Jimmy grinned. "Sure. Six hundred people, maybe. Got a school and everything."

"I don't remember seeing it."

"We turned off just before the town to get to Ashkii's place."

"Is the missing person from Shonto?"

Jimmy nodded. "He lives beyond Shonto up toward Last End Wash. The road there is why we need the Bronco." He slowed to make the turn at the intersection of Route 98. "The missing man is named Curtis Peaches. His girlfriend called it in, said he'd been gone for two days now. He went out to check on their goats, after that planned to take a walk. He didn't come back that night. When he hadn't returned the next morning she began to worry, but it wasn't the first time he'd stayed away for a while. But today she became concerned enough to call."

"Did he have a weapon with him?" Zack asked.

"She says no."

Jimmy turned right at the intersection with the road to Shonto. Zack recognized the turnoff for Route 221 and the murder scene as they roared by. Almost immediately after that the town of Shonto appeared. He saw blocks of housing developments not so different from places in Maryland he had known except for the lack of green lawns and trees. The Preparatory School dominated the town.

Jimmy drove right through Shonto. All at once the town was behind them and the pavement turned to dirt. They rolled along on a dusty road headed north through an arid landscape of short pine trees, sage and cacti, scattered as if from a pepper shaker. Bony humps of bare sandstone rose up once in a while like turtle's backs. It was hot.

They came to a 'Y' intersection. Zack saw no sign or route identification, but Jimmy took the left fork without hesitating. The road was well maintained, level, and smooth. The ride was actually comfortable until Jimmy steered the Bronco off the road, across the ditch and into a pair of ruts. It was apparent now why Jimmy had chosen the Bronco. The track ran through thickening brush then pitched steeply upward onto bare sandstone. No sign of the road was visible until they reached the top where the sandstone ended and ruts reappeared. With a cascading roar of its engine the little Bronco crested the summit and churned on. A few minutes later, a grove of trees came into view. Zack saw a traditional hogan with a barn nearby and a small shed. A fence made with rough-hewn posts and wire surrounded the shed area. As they drew near they heard the bleating of goats.

Jimmy stopped the Bronco fifty feet from the hogan and turned off the engine. They waited until the door of the home opened and a woman appeared and held the door wide, inviting them. As they walked toward the building, Zack noticed the care someone had taken of the plantings alongside the home. Several varieties of cacti were flowering, wisps of a grassy plant waved with the breeze and twinkled with tiny pink flowers, tall sunflowers aimed their yellow faces east. The path to the door was graveled and lined. The hogan was constructed of traditional log and mud plaster and was well kept up.

"Yá'át'ééh!" Introductions were made, and the woman stood by the doorway holding the screen for them. She was dressed in the traditional Navajo way. Her skirt was decorated in turquoise and red flowers and her white blouse had ruffles at the sleeve and the neck. A large stone necklace hung over the blouse. Black hair, brown skin, a face of unusual elegance was Zack's impression as he swept by her and went on in. The interior of the home was as carefully appointed as the exterior had suggested it would be.

Jimmy introduced himself in Navajo. He pointed to Zack and continued speaking in their native tongue. Zack understood the phrase "FBI Agent Tolliver" but that was all. After a few more sentences, Jimmy turned to him and spoke in English. "This is Morning Flower. She is of the Towering House people." He quickly added," Don't worry about clan relationships for now, but you will need to know them. Her missing boyfriend is called Curtis Peaches, his surname is Benally."

The woman nodded, waved them to a seat on the couch. A large colorful rug covered the floor in front of it. Other carpets overlapped around the entirety of the floor.

"Iced tea?" she asked. She spoke with the hesitancy of one not fluent in English.

"Please," Zack said and smiled.

Jimmy nodded.

The kitchen was through a door off the living room. Zack could see a corner of it and glimpses of his hostess as she moved from fridge to counter. The noise of a generator surged with the opening and closing of the fridge.

The men waited silently until she appeared with two glasses, ice cubes clinking, a sprig of mint on top.

Jimmy asked a polite question in Navajo, she waved him off. She wasn't having tea, she wanted them to go ahead and drink. After the first sip, Jimmy made the usual enquiries in English about the weather; had the nights been cold? He complemented her home. The goats seemed healthy. Was the corn crop coming in well?

With each question Morning Flower answered him in stilted but understandable English. Zack was impatient to get to the matter at hand, but he understood and appreciated the custom that demanded pleasantries first.

Finally, Jimmy asked about Curtis.

Morning Flower repeated what they already knew.

"How was he dressed when he left?" Jimmy asked.

She thought a moment. "Jeans, shirt, and hat. He always wore his brown boots." She paused for a moment, thinking. "He did not take his wool jacket. If he knew he might be late, he would take it."

Zack remembered the murder victim did not have a jacket.

"Did he take his rifle?" Jimmy asked.

Morning Flower gave him a puzzled look. "No. When he goes for a walk he never takes a rifle."

"Do you have a picture of him?"

She stood, walked to a table at the far wall and brought back a framed photo. Jimmy looked at it, passed it on to Zack. It showed a cowboy leaning against a fence, his arm around a woman, easily seen to be Morning Flower. The cowboy had his hat low over his brow, his face half in shadow.

Zack could not tell if the man in the photo was the shooting victim.

Jimmy handed the photo back to her. "Do you have any other pictures?"

She shook her head. "Curtis does not like cameras. He is too impatient to pose."

"Where is his vehicle?" Jimmy asked.

"He does not drive."

60

Jimmy considered that. "We will issue an alert for him," he said. "The police will be on watch. Agent Tolliver and I will try to follow his tracks from here."

They walked to the door, she held it and watched them. Zack was impressed with this woman, her poise, her class. Not once had she become insistent or broken down emotionally, yet Zack could see the distress under the surface. He felt a strong desire to find her man for her.

Zack glanced around at the wide expanse of the plateau. "Where on earth do you plan to start?"

Jimmy reached into the Bronco and extracted a rifle. "Over there," he said. "She said he went to check on the goats first. That's where we can begin tracking." The goats greeted them gleefully. Jimmy reached into a bin at the shed and brought out a large scoop of feed. "Don't know how much they've been fed since Curtis left," he said, spreading the feed in the yard with a long sweep of his arm. "Can't hurt to top it off."

They walked around the goat pen. On the opposite side from the hogan they found a path leading east through the scattered trees. It looked as if Curtis had taken this path many times.

They followed the path up a slight rise. Some boot prints looked fresh even to Zack's unpracticed eye.

"He's walking steadily here, with purpose," Jimmy said. They followed the path for the next ten minutes, Jimmy in the lead, occasionally leaning close to the ground to see better, moving on. Now he stopped, knelt.

"Look at this," he said. He put two fingers in the indentation of a boot print. "He stopped here, then turned and stood a while looking back. This print is deeper than the rest."

"Resting?"

Jimmy shook his head. "He doesn't need to rest. It's as if he's watching to be sure he wasn't followed." He studied the prints, shaking his head slowly. "This man isn't out for a meandering walk, he has a purpose."

They kept on. Trees thickened around them, pinyon and juniper. The footprints continued. When the ground began to change, shedding its soil and leaving a smooth patina of sandstone it became harder to locate prints.

"We must be nearing the embankment of the wash," Jimmy said.

"What wash?"

"The Shonto Wash is up ahead. There is high ground at the edge of the wash. Beyond that it's barren, very few trees."

As Jimmy suspected, they came to a steep embankment with a grand vista out over a wide flat area of stone and dirt. The bank was not precipitous, but it was fifty feet above the level of the dry runoff. Curtis' boot prints were obvious where he had clambered down the soft soil.

Zack stared across the wide bed to the far mesas blue with distance. "Where is Shonto from here?"

Jimmy pointed in a southeast direction.

"And where is Ashkii's place?"

He moved his arm slightly north.

"How far is that?"

"Maybe three, maybe four miles, longer by road." Jimmy squinted at Zack. "You're thinking Curtis could have gone all the way there?"

"Aren't you?"

Jimmy shrugged. "Let's climb down and see what we can learn."

They descended quickly. Zack's shoes filled with sand. He envied Jimmy his tall boots. At the bottom the soft sandy soil of the wash held clear footprints. A tangle of older prints told them this was not the first time Curtis had come this way.

Jimmy knelt and ran his fingers over the depressions. "The imprints here are deeper than those going forward. Curtis stood here a while, as if scanning the terrain ahead. He must have seen something or been looking for something." Jimmy looked forward. "Now he's moving faster, confident." The Navajo moved faster as well, almost as if he were right behind the imaginary man they were tracking. Then he stopped.

The ground beneath them was a chaotic mass of impressions, flattened in a wide area, indented and gouged as if someone had rolled about. Zack saw the paw prints of a large animal.

"What happened here?" he asked.

Jimmy was still working the puzzle. After viewing from several angles, kneeling, touching he said, "It came from over there." He pointed in the direction Curtis' tracks had been heading. "It charged him, knocked him to the ground. See here where its toes imprinted deep as it made its leap." His pointing finger followed the story written on the ground. "They fought, wrestled, thrashed around. The man broke free here"—Jimmy pointed beyond the disturbed earth—"and ran, the beast after him. See how its paw prints are on top of the boot prints." They followed a short distance and came to the side of a road. Here they found another confusion of boots and paws and then— nothing.

CHAPTER NINE

Zack leaned forward in his chair, the conversation meaningless to him, conducted entirely in Navajo. Morning Flower's face was ashen. She stared at Jimmy Chaparral's countenance as if to memorize every feature, sinking back into the couch cushions as if to escape his words.

Zack knew the difficulty Jimmy must be having as he tried to explain what they had found—or rather hadn't found; Curtis' footprints ending out there, never to continue. The huge animal prints. The sandy ground so disturbed, the flight. The trail ending at the road. And then he was gone.

It seemed to Zack as if the scenario Jimmy described was the one thing Morning Flower feared most, almost as if she had anticipated it.

Jimmy had little to say to Zack as they drove away from Morning Flower's house. His face was grim. To Zack's questions his only response was, "You saw the evidence."

Now as the Bronco bounced in and out of ruts, Zack tried again. "What did Morning Flower say? Did she have any idea what it all means?"

Jimmy darted a glance at Zack. "No more than you or me, according to her. You just graduated from a great academy where they teach this sort of thing. What did your education tell you happened out there?"

"I have no idea. I don't even know what kind of animal that was."

"It was a huge canine, like a wolf or dog."

"A dog!"

"My report will say the man went for a walk, was attacked by a huge canine, ran for his life pursued by the creature, and both disappeared at the roadway, possibly entering a vehicle." He glanced at Zack. "That is not what my people will say. My people will say Curtis Peaches was taken by a witch. That is what Morning Flower believes."

Zack stared at Jimmy. "A witch? That's craziness."

Jimmy was quiet for the next few minutes. He glanced at Zack. "This case is mine. This will not fall under federal jurisdiction, not without a body. We have no evidence to draw a connection between Curtis' disappearance and the murder."

"What will you do, then?"

"Just what the feds would do. We'll get scent dogs out there and try to find out what happened to Curtis. We'll search the entire area. We'll talk to people to learn who may have wanted to harm him."

"What will you say to people who believe it was a witch?"

Jimmy gave a wry grin. "I will give everyone what they want and expect."

At Elk Wells, Jimmy left Zack at the black Ford and went to his office to collect men for the search. Zack drove back to Tuba City to report to his boss.   When the bell clanged at his entrance to the reception area, the girl behind the counter looked up with a big smile.

"Hello again, Agent."

"Hello, Miss..."

"Bistie. Bella Bistie."

"Please call me Zack."

"Is this a come-on?" she asked, her smile now teasing.

Zack was on more familiar ground now. Flirtation was the same, east or west. "Sure, if you want it to be."

She cocked her head to one side. "You know what they say about dating work colleagues?"

"No, what?"

"Yes."

"Ahem!" A cough interrupted their conversation.

Ben stood at the doorway to the offices. "Maybe you have time to hang around out here, Agent Tolliver, but I have work to do."

"Yes, sir." Zack turned to follow him through the door.

"I have you in my program now, Zack," Bella called after him.

He waved as he left the room. Had he just made a date? Is that what just happened? Or did she simply mean the metal detector programming? Or both?

Zack was still puzzling over this as he followed Ben through the door. Ben's office was not as neat as on his first visit. Several books had been pulled down off shelves, a map was spread on the carpeted floor. His desk was piled with paper.

He waved Zack to the chair. "I've had a brief from Sergeant Chaparral's office. Now I'd like to hear about the missing man case from you."

Zack began with meeting Morning Flower. After he relayed what she had said, he described tracking Curtis to the cliffs. Then he described the scene of the apparent attack and possible abduction.

Ben had sat silent, hands clasped on his desk, eyes intent on Zack. He did not interrupt. When Zack stopped, he said, "Hmmm" and pushed a button on the desk phone.

"Yes, sir?" Bella's voice lilted from the speaker.

"Bella, please find Eagle Feather. I need to speak to him."

"I'll try, sir. But you know how that goes."

"Do your best. I need him ASAP."

Ben hung up the phone, looked at Zack. "I'll have Eagle Feather go have a look."

Zack cocked an eyebrow. "You think he might find something Jimmy missed?"

Ben shrugged. "Always the possibility. Sergeant Chaparral is a good tracker. Eagle Feather is the best tracker in these parts."

"Is he an FBI agent?"

"Oh, no. He's just a hunting guide. Because of his skills, we have a loose arrangement whereby he helps us out in between clients."

"Like picking me up at the airport?"

"That too."

Ben smiled suddenly. "That reminds me, you'll need these." He opened a desk drawer and withdrew a ring of keys, a pager, and a keycard. He held up the keys. "These are your office keys, and vehicle keys. We have a Jeep you can use. And, of course, the Ford." He picked up the keycards. "This lets you through the security door along with the camera that recognizes your facial image. It also lets you into our little lab in the back." He stood. "Let's go take a look at your new office."

Zack followed Ben out into the corridor. There were two more doors along the hall and one at the end with a large glass window. Ben opened the first door on the left, next to his own office. He stood aside for Zack to enter.

The office was about the same size as Ben's but seemed larger without the bookshelves. There was a solid metal desk with telephone, computer, in-and-out trays. Next to the desk was a small table with a printer. The floor was carpeted in beige.

"You'll figure out what you need as time goes on," Ben said. "Meanwhile, let's get right to work. There is a report there from our forensic work at the murder site." He waved toward the desk surface. "Take a look at it, give it a think. Regarding the missing man case, keep up to date with Sergeant Chaparral. If it is determined to be a murder, it will be your first case." He grinned. "Unless, of course, it is connected to my murder." He turned away. "I'll leave you to it." He shut the door behind him.

Zack went behind his new desk and sat down in the comfortable swivel chair. He looked around the room with a feeling of pride. His first real job. His first office. He looked down at the desk top. His first task.

Zack read the report. The victim was as yet unidentified, male, age about forty-five. The cause of death was a single gunshot wound to the abdomen, the bullet entering the back left side of the spine and exiting below the rib cage. Approximate time of death was eight to twelve hours before discovery.

He glanced down at the next item, the recovered rifle slug from Jimmy Chaparral's gun under the coyote. He saw that the rifling identification was consistent with the rifle Jimmy used, no surprise. They did find flesh and blood traces on the slug. It was sent out for testing and determined to be animal, not human. More specifically, canine. More specific than that would take more time.

Item three was a report on the sheep mutilation from an FBI forensics specialist on temporary duty at Tuba City. He believed the sheep died from severing of the carotid artery and both jugular veins with a deep incision from a sharp narrow implement, identified as the razor knife found with the victim's body. The eyes were removed with the same instrument. The stomach cavity was opened with the same instrument. The contents of the stomach cavity were left on the ground. The blood on the razor knife belonged to the sheep. There were no identifiable finger prints on the knife.

Zack called Jimmy Chaparral on his cell phone.

"Sergeant Chaparral," came the formal response.

"Hi, Jimmy. Where are you now?"

"I'm in Shonto doing a little house to house. What's up?"

"A couple of things. First, according to our forensics man, while the murder victim could have lived a while after he was shot, they believe he was killed at the scene. The stomach was perforated but yawing of the projectile was minimal, meaning less damage than might have been. To my mind there could still be a connection between the murder victim and our missing man. If you can get a good photo of Curtis we can put that one to rest right away, one way or the other. Blood testing from your rifle bullet is back. They concur you shot a canine. They have not found the bullet that killed the murder victim, so I'm afraid in Agent Witherspoon's mind you are not quite in the clear yet."

He heard Jimmy's laugh. "Yeah, I was expecting that one." There was a pause. "Anything else?"

"Our man says the sheep was killed by a man with knowledge of sheep anatomy."

"So no help. That's pretty much everyone on the Rez." He went right on. "Okay, I'll get a photo of Curtis Peaches and message it to you." He rang off.

Zack sat for a minute, thoughts wandering. As his eye passed over the blank walls, he felt a new rush of excitement. His own office. He thought about what he might hang on the blank walls. He knew he'd want a large map of the Reservation."

His phone rang, interrupting his thoughts. It was Ben.

"Zack, I just heard from Eagle Feather. He's headed up toward Last End Wash to talk to Morning Flower and try to help track her missing man. Meanwhile, he had some news. He backtracked our shooting victim. He says the trail led him back to the road. He believes the killer and his victim arrived together in a vehicle, from the tire tread type and size likely a 4x4 truck. There was no sign of a struggle anywhere. The only footprints belonged to the victim. Eagle Feather thinks the killer never got out of the car."

"How could the killer not leave the car?"

"Well, according to Eagle Feather, the deceased ran from that spot. The killer waited for his shot, took it, and drove away."

Zack pictured it. "Like shooting trophies on safari. He was killing for sport."

"Maybe."

Zack's mind whirled with implications. "The killer must have known the area."

"Maybe."

"So obviously, if the victim came in a vehicle, Jimmy couldn't have shot him while up on the cliff with me. If Eagle Feather is right about this, it means we can let Sergeant Chaparral off the hook."

Zack listened to silence as Ben paused.

"It does not eliminate the possibility that Jimmy brought the murder victim there in his vehicle at an earlier time. And remember, the victim would have been easier to coax into the car of a policeman."

"He'd have to have done all that between the time he brought Jay Begay in to jail and when he picked me up in Tuba City that evening. Seems impossible."

Ben's voice was calm, reasoning. "What better alibi?" He paused. "Look, Zack, our investigation is wide open. I'm simply putting forward the argument I know Scott Witherspoon will propose. Of course, we have to consider every possibility until we have more evidence. I've known Jimmy a long time, naturally I don't really think he's guilty. But my feelings don't count." He paused again. "Of course, Scott Witherspoon seems convinced he's involved somehow. He's bothered by the coincidence of Sergeant Chaparral being up there at about the right time discharging a rifle of a similar type that killed the man. The fact that he had you there as a witness just adds fuel to the fire for him. Jimmy won't be in the clear until we find the real killer."

CHAPTER TEN

After Ben rang off, Zack leaned back in his chair and let his mind chew on the new evidence. He knew Eagle Feather's interpretation of the events would not completely exonerate Jimmy, but neither would Agent Witherspoon's theory implicate him. The truth would come out sooner or later.

The idea the murderer had brought his victim to the scene of his death by car brought new possibilities to mind. Where had they come from? Was it possible to connect Curtis Peaches, the man who coincidently went missing at just the right time, to the cliff-top murder?

Zack turned on the computer on his desk, found the internet browser and searched for a map of the area around Shonto. He moved his cursor to the approximate location of Morning Flower's hogan and from there to the place where Curtis disappeared. He found the road where the tracks of man and large canine had ended. From that point, it would be possible to drive to Shonto and from there to the old trading post and beyond to the crime scene. Could the killer have used a huge wolf-dog to attack and drive his victim to his truck? If so, how had he subdued Curtis? How had he separated animal and victim without ever stepping out of the truck? The entire scenario refused to jell in his mind.

The desk phone rang. It was Ben.

"Dinnertime, Zack. Let me show you where I like to eat."

The black Ford was out front. Zack climbed in and to his surprise Ben drove to the restaurant where Zack had eaten breakfast, next to the Quality Inn. It was named the Hogan Family Restaurant.

"Is this the only place in town?" Zack asked.

Ben grinned. "Not quite. There's actually a quite good Chinese restaurant, a pizza place, and several fast food stores. But this is where you get a real family style meal." He turned off the ignition and winked at Zack. "And good Mexican."

At Ben's recommendation Zack experienced Fry bread for the first time, which to him tasted like donut treats from childhood. Ben explained it was a recipe of necessity for the Navajo when their only provisions came from the U.S. Government during the early days on the reservation. "There was just so much you could do with flour, salt, baking soda, and a bit of oil. But add sugar or syrup and it's quite tasty."

Zack had to agree.

When the discussion came around to the murder case, Zack offered his thought that it might be connected to the missing man case.

Ben shook his head. "I doubt it. You've just arrived here. You see two disturbing situations that occur about the same time in more or less the same area and you say, 'Hey, they must be connected.' What you don't see is how often these things happen. People on the Reservation go missing all the time. A father may just decide to move on, and off he goes without a word. A kid decides to try life in California for a while, and off he goes." He picked up his water glass.

Zack couldn't help himself. "Do people vanish in thin air a lot?"

Ben raised an eyebrow. A thickset, solidly built man, his manner was unflappable. "No more than in most American cities." He took another sip of his water. "Again, Zack, you're new here. These people are Navajo. They are skilled, completely at home in this environment. Many of them could decide to lay down a set of tracks to nowhere and disappear. It takes an Indian to find an Indian, as they say. Let Eagle Feather do his work, and we'll see."

After the meal, after Ben had graciously picked up the tab, Zack stood in the parking lot and watched the black Ford drive away, calmed by the earthy smells and subdued sounds of the early evening in this strange place. In Virginia, the roar of traffic was ever present, the smell of diesel mixed with fast food smells hung in the air. He turned and walked to the entrance of the Quality Inn. Inside the lobby, a young woman rose from a stuffed armchair in the waiting area.

Bella Bistie wore a mischievous smile, her dark eyes glistening with humor. Her black hair was unwrapped now and hung over her shoulders. In place of the quite proper high-buttoned white collared shirt and black tassel bowtie of earlier in the day she wore an embroidered puffed-sleeved collarless blouse, one shoulder bared, with a long turquoise bead necklace. Her white gathered skirt came just below the knees and around her slim waist she wore a brown braided sash and Concho belt. To Zack, she was an image of beauty.

"I'm here for our date," she said.

Zack could only stare.

"Have you changed your mind?"

"Uh, no! Yes! I mean, I wasn't sure..."

She laughed. Her teeth were sparkling white against bright red lipstick. "Don't worry, I'm teasing you. But I do want to show you around the town. I see it as my duty as administrative secretary."

"Well, then, I'm all yours. Do I need a jacket?"

"No. We're not going far." She slipped her arm in his elbow and tugged him back out the motel door. They walked toward Hogan's Restaurant.

Zack looked at her, eyebrows raised. "I just came from here."

She smiled. "I know. Ben told me he'd be bringing you here. But we're going to Hogan Espresso, not the restaurant." She dragged him along. "It's the best place to see the young people of Tuba City, especially tonight."

Zack had trouble keeping pace with her. "Why especially tonight?"

She grinned. "It's Open Mic Night."

Uh-oh, Zack thought.

They stopped in the coffee shop to look at the dessert display case.

"Ooh, they have carrot cake!" Bella looked at Zack. "Buy us some. This is the best!"

Out on the deck, at a patio table, Zack had to agree. He took another bite and washed it down with decaf. Darkness had crept in while they were in line for their food, now lamps had come on around the deck. A tech guy was busy with set-up on a platform next to the building wall.

"This is exciting," Zack said. "It feels like opening night around here."

"Everybody enjoys these nights," Bella said. "There are a lot of people here with talent. You'll see."

They chatted like old friends. Every so often Bella would leap up and scamper to another table to greet people she knew. Other young Navajos stopped by the table to see her. The place hummed with activity.

When bright spotlights flashed on and illuminated the platform, everyone returned to their seats and conversations died down. A man in a white cowboy hat and tinted glasses stepped to the microphone.

" Yá'át'ééh ałní'íní ," he said, his voice booming out over the system. "Good evening, y'all. Welcome to all you who are travelin' through and welcome back all you Homies and Homegirls." He sang to the tune from the beer commercial, 'Tonight is kinda special.'

"Yeah, that's right, we got some great talent lined up tonight an' you're not gonna want to miss a single moment, so fasten your safety belts cause here we go!" He looked at a paper in his hand. "First up is Lisa Tso singing and strumming the six string doin' her own song "I Missed Midnight." Let's give it up for Lisa! Hey-Oh!"

The young girl was surprisingly good, her voice soft and soothing, the nylon strings and wistful minor chords evoking a haunting moment. The applause was loud.

Act followed act, from rap to poetry, mime to comedy routines. It seemed the entire community had talent and wanted to share it. The evening flew by. Many curious glances came Zack's way. He guessed word had spread about the new FBI recruit. Likely most had heard the story of his very un-FBI-like appearance at Jay Begay's arrest. Bella seemed to enjoy the covert glances.

THE DARK ROAD

The moment came when the announcer looked their way and called Bella's name. Zack watched her stride to the platform and remove the microphone from its stand. The gathering appeared to know what was coming and everyone applauded wildly. She cued the tech guy who started up a recording. After a soft intro she began to sing in sultry alto a song Zack hadn't heard before. It was very lyric and plaintive, performed in a Marlene Dietrich style, in German. After the first verse she traveled with the mic into the audience, singing table to table. Everyone was entranced. She worked her way to Zack and sang directly to him. He didn't understand a single word.

Bella ended the song, the accompaniment faded, she handed the microphone to the techie who appeared beside her, and sat down to thunderous applause. As the announcer presented the next act, Bella gave Zack a triumphant grin.

He raised his eyebrows. "You are full of surprises."

Her smile broadened.

When the show ended, Bella had one more thing to show Zack. She led him to her yellow Toyota pickup and they drove north out of the town. At a place where the road ascended some bluffs she pulled over and they stepped out. It was completely dark, but Bella seemed to know the ground well. She took Zack's hand and led him up a path to the top of the knoll. There she stopped, said nothing.

Zack looked around. He saw tiny lights winking here and there, house lights in the distance, he guessed. But the real show was above him. The stars shone so brightly it seemed they were lighting the land around him like a zillion tiny flashlights. He'd never seen so many stars.

Bella watched his face. "You don't have this back east, do you."

"No, we don't," Zack breathed.

"Do you see that star just above and a little in front that glows so bright?"

Zack knew which one she meant. "The North Star, right?"

"We call it the Northern Fire. It is surrounded by four other stars. Náhookos Biko,' 'Central Fire in the Sky,' represents the fire in the center of the hogan, and Náhookos Bika'ii and Náhookos Bi'áadii circle around it. Together, all three constellations represent the family. Do you see it?"

"I see four stars around it, yes."

She laughed. "It helps to be familiar with the figures, see them in your mind."

"I see the Big Dipper," Zack offered.

"We call it Náhookos Bika'ii," she said. "Do you see? He is lying on his side, slightly raised on his left elbow. He represents the father and protector of the home."

Zack was aware of her closeness as she leaned in toward him, pointing and speaking in hushed tones. "I think I can see it."

"In the name of gender equality, look at the constellation you call Cassiopeia, over there." She pointed. "We call it Náhookos Bi'áadii. It is a woman lying on her side. She represents the woman of the home."

"Yes, I see that." Zack's neck was beginning to feel the strain.

"There, now," Bella said with a giggle. "You already know three Navajo Sky People. You are practically Navajo yourself."

Zack felt an overpowering urge to hold this girl. Something about the perfume she wore, the primitive smell of the arid land at night, maybe too many decafs—he felt like a schoolboy with a crush.

As if sensing his feelings, Bella stepped away. "We'd better get home. Ben will be unhappy if we both come in tired and cranky tomorrow." She laughed again, took his hand, and led him down the path.

Zack followed sheep-like. When they reached the truck, he opened her door for her, closed it and turned to go around to the passenger side. Something made him glance back up the hill they had just climbed down. He stopped short and stared.

A figure stood in the path above him, fifty feet away, visible somehow despite the darkness. It was a man, an Indian, with long black braids and piercing dark eyes. He wore an open collar flannel shirt and blue jeans tucked into scuffed boots, a white cowboy hat on his head. The man's eyes were intent upon something beyond Zack, his face was contorted with an expression somewhere between anger and despair. As Zack stared, the man slowly faded away, as if absorbed cell by cell into the darkness.

Bella had started the truck, now she rolled down the window. "Are you coming or what?"

CHAPTER ELEVEN

Zack said nothing about the apparition to Bella, or anyone else for that matter. He figured he was off to a shaky enough start as the butt of humor at the Begay arrest and didn't need to add to that perception. He was perpetually tired, immersed in a different culture in a new landscape. He was probably lucky not to see pink elephants behind every bush.

Bella had dropped him off at the hotel last night and marched straight to his room, climbed into bed and fell into a deep sleep. He was sitting at a small table at Hogan's next morning sipping coffee and anticipating his first normal start to the day at the office when someone slid into the chair opposite him.

" Yá'át'ééh, White Man."

Zack looked at the sphinxlike face of Eagle Feather.

"Hello..."

"Go ahead, enjoy your breakfast. I will talk while you eat."

A pile of yellow scrambled eggs arrived at that moment. Zack obeyed.

"Ben has said you will work with Jimmy on the Curtis Peaches case and so I should talk to you. I have spoken with Morning Flower. I have followed your tracks into the Shonto Wash."

Zack's fork was part way to his mouth. "You saw what happened there?"

Eagle Feather nodded.

Zack stared at him, chewing. "The dog attack. The abduction."

Eagle Feather's eyes showed a glint of humor. "Did Jimmy say the man was attacked?"

Zack nodded. "Yes."

Eagle Feather studied him as if weighing his response. "White Man, when you read sign you can see with these"—he pointed to his eyes—"or you can see with this"—he pointed to his heart. "It is important to know how to do it with both."

Zack angled his head. "I don't follow."

"You saw what your brain programmed you to see. You followed the tracks of a man walking alone. Below the cliff, you found the man tracks approached by large canine tracks. Where they joined you saw disturbed earth, signs of a struggle. The man ran, the animal pursued. Then both man and animal tracks disappeared."

Zack shook his head slowly. "Yes, both disappeared at the road. That's what we said."

Eagle Feather arched an eyebrow. "When you followed the man's footprints, you knew he was missing. You knew that was not a good thing. You thought this with your brain, you felt it with your heart. When you saw the animal tracks approach, you continued to think with your heart, and so you chose to believe the evil rather than the good." Eagle Feather put a long brown finger on the table between them. "You saw what is possible, but not all that is possible. You did not think anything good was possible."

Zack's fork paused in midair. "Nothing good could have happened. It's impossible."

"It is not only possible, it is probable." Eagle Feather stood, looked down at Zack for a moment, turned and walked away.

Zack stared after him, his appetite gone. His mind was in chaos by what this man seemed to be telling him. It was absurd. Jimmy Chaparral was there, had led the way, seen the tracks, described the attack. He too was a Navajo, a good tracker by all reports. He had seen what Zack saw, a man attacked by a beast.

But he remembered what Jimmy said later, about how the Dine' would choose to believe this mysterious animal was a witch. He remembered watching as Jimmy spoke to Morning Flower in their language, saw how devastated she had become at his words. What had he told her, actually? All they knew then was what she had already known, that Curtis Peaches was missing. But during that interview her face had shown despair, almost horror. Had Jimmy told her something else, something she found harder to face? Was Jimmy keeping his real suspicions from Zack?

When Zack started his career with the FBI none of his imaginings had included dealing with ghostly miscreants you couldn't even identify, let alone put into handcuffs. Zack stared into his half-finished cup of coffee. He thought about Sergeant Chaparral's response when Zack asked him how he would deal with the expectations of his Navajo people, remembered how he said he would give everyone what they wanted and expected. Zack had no knowledge or experience with Navajo mysticism, therefore that was not an option for him. But he was trained in step by step procedures and the rules of evidence and that was how he must proceed, whether people saw ghosts or not.

That settled, Zack felt more comfortable. He paid for his breakfast and walked down the street to his new office in a better frame of mind, humming a tune.

The tune died on his lips when he sat down at his desk and opened a large envelope left there by Jimmy Chaparral. It was a picture of the missing man, Curtis Peaches, standing next to a sheep pen, smiling at the camera. He wore a flannel shirt of blue and red plaid, blue jeans tucked into scuffed boots, braids of long black hair and a cowboy hat. In this photo his face was clearly visible. It was the man Zack had seen the night before, the apparition. He dropped the photo on the desk as if it was hot and continued to stare at it.

After overcoming his shock, he realized the photo just might resolve another question; the man who was murdered on the mesa beyond the Shonto Trading Post had facial features similar to Curtis Peaches. The missing man might no longer be missing.

Zack called Jimmy to tell him, but the Navajo stopped him midsentence.

"Hold on," Jimmy said. "Let's not do this over the phone. Can you meet me in Kate's Cafe in Elk Wells?"

"Half an hour," Zack said.

"And, Zack? Please don't talk to anyone else."

"But I've got to tell Ben, show him the photo. It's new evidence."

"Zack, it won't hurt to wait on that a bit. Look, there are sensitive issues involved here. Once the feds get their teeth into it, they're like bulldogs. I won't be able to protect the sensitivities of my people. Now that we believe the cases are connected, we can choose the best time for all concerned to hand it over. Let's talk first, pretend I haven't quite sent the photo. Remember, I'm the one in charge of this particular case."

Zack reluctantly agreed. He checked in with Ben, who barely looked up from his desk, told Bella where he'd be, and went around back of the building with the Jeep keys dangling from his finger. The sun was strong, the day warming, and Zack folded back the roof of the Jeep. It started with a happy six cylinder 4.0 liter roar. Zack spun it around the lot once, liked what he felt, and headed out. Twenty minutes later he approached Elk Wells, Hank Williams singing in his ears. This time he felt he belonged in his surroundings.

He found Jimmy seated at a table at Kate's. To Zack's surprise, someone else was there with him, the ephemeral Eagle Feather. The two Navajo watched him approach, Jimmy smiling, Eagle Feather stone-faced.

Jimmy kicked out a chair for Zack. "We didn't want you to say too much over an open line. We can talk here without being overheard."

Zack frowned. "My FBI line is not secure?"

"A telephone line is a telephone line. No federal budget is going to invest in expensive scrambling devices for your little liaison office."

Zack was still puzzled. "Who is going to care about this case beyond people on the Reservation?"

"That is a good question," Eagle Feather said.

Jimmy looked at Eagle Feather, turned back to Zack. "I've been searching for background on Curtis Peaches. Morning Flower has known him less than a year, he moved in with her just a couple of months ago. She could tell me nothing of the man's past before she met him. I had Lenana do a search in every data bank she could access. No one named Curtis Peaches, Curtis Benally, Peaches Benally, or any combination exists on any record she could find." He tapped the table with his finger. "Lenana is very good at what she does." He went on. "I checked with Morning Flower's neighbors and asked everyone I could speak with in Shonto about Curtis, showed them the picture, but no one knew anything about him. It's like his background was erased."

"People without backgrounds are hiding from something or someone," Eagle Feather said. "He acts like one who is being hunted."

"Where did he live prior to moving in with Morning Flower?" Zack asked.

"She says he lived in an old trailer out toward Last End Wash, tended a herd of sheep up that way," Jimmy said. "He gave up the job when he moved in with Morning Flower. I was up to that trailer once, long time now. It was deserted back then. Curtis might have just helped himself, no one would have noticed or cared. Morning Flower found the photo I sent you among his things. She'd never seen it before. It looks like it was taken at Last End Wash, before she met him. We don't know who the photographer was." He glanced at Eagle Feather. "There is one other thing she said that I haven't told you. She told me he had a lot of money with him when he came to live with her. He helped her fix up the place, never told her where he got it."

Zack raised his eyebrows at that. "Not likely from tending sheep."

Jimmy gave a wry grin. "Not likely."

Zack looked at Eagle Feather. "But what happened to him? Where did the large canine come from? How did he end up dead above the cliffs? And why?"

Eagle Feather nodded. "We do have much to learn. The man worked as a shepherd. Shepherds use dogs. If you know someone is hunting you, you want to have a big dog. Was someone hunting him? Is that why he came here?" He paused, looked at Zack. "It is difficult to lose your background so thoroughly. Most people need help."

Jimmy nodded. "Maybe at some point you can ask Ben about that."

Zack looked up in surprise. "You think the FBI knows about Peaches?"

"Sometimes the federal organizations share information among themselves. It certainly wouldn't be the first time the U.S. Marshals, CIA or FBI used the Reservation to hide someone."

CHAPTER TWELVE

Mischievous brown eyes lingered on Zack when he came through the office door. Bella's transition from crooning nightclub heart-stopper to tight-collared and efficient receptionist was almost as mysterious to Zack as the specter of Curtis Peaches. She made a hitchhiking motion with her thumb toward the inner sanctum indicating he was wanted by the boss.

"Am I in trouble?"

"That's between you and your conscience, but Ben wants to see you because the lab tests are in."

Zack whistled. "That was fast." He felt sudden excitement. The test results might confirm the answers to a number of questions.

"Thanks, Bella."

She smiled and buzzed him through the inner door.

Ben's office was open a few inches, as if in expectation. Zack heard conversation inside. He knocked lightly, bringing the conversation to an abrupt stop.

"Come on in, Zack," Ben said.

Zack felt a knot in his stomach at the sight of Agent Scott Witherspoon in a chair next to Ben's desk. Without knowing exactly why, he had begun to dislike this agent from Flagstaff. Ben waved him to an empty chair.

"Scott was kind enough to bring the rifle tests and blood results up from Flagstaff," Ben said. "We have enough in here"— he waved a folder—"to answer most of our questions." He handed the folder to Zack. "Glance through it while we tell you what we know." Ben sat back, his hands a pyramid under his chin.

Zack flipped it open and began reading the columns of data as he listened.

Agent Witherspoon spoke first. "As you know the tissue found on the bullet Sergeant Chaparral allegedly found beneath the coyote was indeed from that animal and was a match for his rifle. We have not yet found the bullet that killed the man on the mesa. Of the two rifles we collected from Chaparral, one had been fired and the other had not. The first was used by Sergeant Chaparral, the second was yours. We cannot confirm how many times Sergeant Chaparral's rifle was fired, but there is just one bullet missing from the magazine. It is confirmed the victim was shot with a rifle of generally similar characteristics. But, of course, that covers a lot of ground."

Ben picked up the narrative. "The blood on the razor knife we found near the victim does indeed match the blood of the mutilated sheep. Unfortunately, there were no identifiable fingerprints on the knife. But the evidence certainly suggests the victim is our sheep mutilator."

There was silence among the three as each eyed the others.

Zack wanted to tell them about the photo but his promise to Jimmy and Eagle Feather held him back. He had a gut feeling he was doing the right thing, but it went against all he had been taught. "So Sergeant Chaparral is in the clear," is all he said, finally.

Agent Witherspoon shifted in his chair to face Zack. "Not so fast. All we have proven is he shot a coyote near the sheep. We can't prove he didn't shoot anyone else, including the murder victim. In addition our forensics expert commented, as you see there, that the shot must have come from a position very similar to the one you and Chaparral occupied.

"But I heard just the one shot. And there was just one bullet missing from his magazine."

Witherspoon smiled at Zack like a teacher patiently teaching a child. "Magazines are exchangeable. And you were asleep, as I remember."

Ben put up a palm. "I don't think we're getting anywhere with this. Let's hold off until we know a bit more." He turned his attention to Zack. "How's that missing man case going?"

Zack had hoped Ben wouldn't ask, especially with Witherspoon in the room. "It's inconclusive at the moment. The man's tracks ended and we haven't been able to pick them up again. Jimmy questioned people at all the nearest residences and anyone who had been in the area, but no luck yet."

"What about Eagle Feather's take on it? Didn't he go up and have a look?"

Zack searched for the right words. "Well, if he had a different take to Sergeant Chaparral's, he didn't tell me what it was."

Ben nodded. "What's your next step?"

Zack leaned forward. "As you know, the case is still in the hands of the Tribal Police. Sergeant Chaparral has arranged for dogs to attempt to track him today."

"That's a lot of territory to cover," Witherspoon said.

"What does the girlfriend—Morning Flower, is it?—think happened to him," Ben asked.

Zack shook his head. "I don't believe she has any idea. She seemed pretty devastated."

Ben nodded and waved a dismissing hand. "Thanks, Zack. Keep me informed, please."

Zack stood, nodded to both men, and escaped out the door and into his office. At his desk, his face flamed red when he thought about the position he'd put himself in. He had information possibly of great consequence to the investigation he had not shared. In fact, he'd been deceptive. The agents did not question who Peaches was or what he was doing there. Was it because the missing person case was of no real importance to them? Or were they being evasive? In any case, some gut instinct told Zack not to share everything while Witherspoon was in the room.

He picked up his desk phone and called Jimmy's cell. After three rings he received a message saying Sergeant Chaparral's phone either off or out of range. He left a message, then tried to turn his mind to the forms and other mundane matters requiring his attention. He found it difficult.

He was glad when Jimmy called just five minutes later. The Navajo policeman wanted to know if Curtis Peaches had any relationship with the feds.

"I haven't asked yet. Agent Witherspoon is with Ben. I'll try later when I can get Ben to myself."

"I think that is wise."

"Is there a problem between the two of you?"

There was a pause. "Let's just say Agent Witherspoon and I disagreed about how to handle a prisoner on one occasion. Can we leave it at that?"

Zack grinned to himself. "Of course."

"You called because...?"

"Right. I wondered if you've arranged for the dogs yet?"

"Yes, I did. Libby—she's the handler—is on her way up there now. Eagle Feather will meet her there, show her the area.

He'll get back to me, but he's pretty sure it's a waste of time, thinks the dog will come to the road and simply whimper." Jimmy sighed. "But one step at a time. I told him just go ahead and let's see what Big Blue can do."

"Big Blue?"

Jimmy laughed. "That's Libby's newest dog. Amazing animal. He can follow a snake through a tar pit. I'll call you as soon as I know anything."

Neither spoke for a moment. "Is there something else?" Jimmy asked.

Zack didn't know how to begin. "This will sound strange, but I saw him last night."

"You saw who?"

"The missing man, the shepherd, Curtis." Zack hesitated. "Not for real, I mean I know he wasn't real, but he looked real. Just as real as you or me. Then he disappeared."

There was a moment of quiet. "Zack, you continue to surprise me. I want to know more about that, but not over the phone. I'll call in a couple of hours."

The moment Zack hung up, he regretted his impulse to tell Jimmy about the apparition. After all, the vision had to be an effect of the mind brought on by the newness and strangeness of his situation. Confessing he'd seen the apparition was the kind of thing could ruin a man's career, like airline pilots confessing to seeing UFOs. Well, he'd followed his impulse and he'd damn well better have been right. For one thing, he needed to learn a lot more about the dead man he'd seen, this Curtis Peaches. He called Jimmy right back.

"Are we some sort of BFF's now?" Jimmy asked.

"I'm sorry to keep at you. I need a favor. I want to go see the place where Curtis lived before he moved in with Morning Flower. Can you show me?"

Jimmy paused. "Wish I could, but I'm in the middle of something, and it's a long way. I'll tell you what, though, come on out here to the station and I'll arrange to have a man guide you up there. That good enough?"

"Couldn't ask for more."

Jimmy chuckled. "Well, I'm sure you could, but you wouldn't get it."

Once again Zack found himself on the Navajo Highway headed east toward Elk Wells with Ben's blessing. It was almost as if Ben enjoyed seeing Zack leave the office. Once again he felt a gnawing in his stomach. His breakfast had not served him as well as it should, particularly after Eagle Feather made his appearance. He planned to see if Katie would make him a sandwich to take along on the drive to Last End Wash.

When he emerged from Katie's Cafe he had his lunch in hand, more of a bag dinner, really—a beef sandwich, banana, cookies, chips, and several sizeable chunks of fry bread. He found a large Ford pickup with a trailer parked outside. Jimmy was inspecting the trailer hitch connections. Zack heard restless clumping noises from the trailer's interior.

"Horses?"

The stocky Navajo policeman with a ruddy face poked his head around from behind the trailer, studied Zack for moment and said, "Yep."

Jimmy stood and stretched with both hands on his back. "Zack, you remember Lané Shorter? I think he was here for the Jay Begay situation."

92

"I remember. Howdy."

Lané nodded, turned back to whatever he had been doing.

"Lané will be your guide up to the Wash."

"Horses?" Zack asked again.

Jimmy smiled. "There's no good road for the last several miles. You do ride, don't you? Didn't they teach you to use anything except cars and motorcycles at that fancy academy?"

Zack grimaced, looking down at his low cut sneakers.

Jimmy laughed. "Those shoes will do just fine." He motioned toward the truck cab. "Climb in. You need to get going or you won't see much before darkness sets in." He gave the back fender a slap as if it was a horse's flank.

Lané slipped behind the wheel and started up the 450-horsepower 3.5 liter EcoBoost engine. It emitted a confident rumbling. Zack didn't know horses, but he did know trucks and he wondered where they could possibly be going that this F-150 Raptor couldn't take them.

They roared out of town and onto Route 160, the road smooth as silk. Route 98, recently paved, was a smooth black ribbon through the baked red soil and scrub brush landscape. They took the road to Shonto, by now quite familiar to Zack. Just beyond the turnoff to the trading post Lané slowed and eased the rig through a sharp left turn, heading west with large housing developments on either side.

As soon as the developments were behind them, all pretense at pavement ended. The road, composed mostly of sand and dirt, continued in a westerly direction. They bumped along through ruts, other times soft sand. The jolting ride kept the horses moving about to keep their balance. Sage brush, rabbit bush, and shrub live oak were scattered randomly across the landscape with the occasional turtleback sandstone ridges rising here and there. At one such ridge the road offered several divisions and a confusing kaleidoscope of ruts. Lané didn't hesitate, shifted the Ford into a lower gear and powered up the side of the sandstone face. On the far side, just as the trailer teetered ominously, the road leveled off and turned back to dirt ruts, now headed north.

Occasional high points offered vistas which brought home to Zack the emptiness of the land around them. He saw scrub, sand, and sky everywhere he looked for as far as he could see. As they jolted along the terrain grew rougher, the rock mounds steeper, and gullies slashed the landscape. After a hard right turn with the trailer barely able to follow they took a dusty track and came to a large rock escarpment. At its foot several trees gave shade and the ground was level. Zack noticed tracks from all-terrain vehicle tires everywhere. He suspected his horseback adventure was about to begin.

He was right.

CHAPTER THIRTEEN

Lané levered open the rear of the trailer and gently slapped his
way between the large rumps, disappeared then reappeared
backing both horses down the ramp with an assurance that left no
doubt he'd done this a few hundred times before. He handed the
reins of a small but sturdy looking Pinto mare to Zack. Her brown
eyes assessed him with long lashes that gave her a coquettish look.

"Her name is Babe," Lané said. He tied his own mount, a
black quarter horse named Mystic dancing with nervous energy, to
the truck tailgate. He tugged a large satchel of supplies out of the
truck bed, then locked the truck. He glanced at Zack while tying
the supply bag behind his saddle.

"Go ahead, mount her, walk her, get used to each other.
She is gentle like a grandmother."

Zack remembered how his own grandmother had her less-
than-gentle moments. He let the mare nuzzle him, stroked her
forelock, and moved slowly to the saddle, keeping a reassuring
palm on her. Then he grasped the pommel, put his foot in stirrup,
and swung up.

"You have ridden before." Zack detected relief in Lané's
voice. He was probably happy not to babysit a novice rider.

Zack circled Babe left and right and found her responsive
and eager to please. He patted her neck. "I don't ride a lot," he
said. "But I do enjoy horses."

Lané was mounted by now. "That is good." He nudged
the black and led off.

Zack had an epiphany. After three and one half days of
uncertainty, never in control, never quite knowing where he was

going or what he might be about to do, not even knowing where he might rest his head for the night, he was experiencing an unexpected peace within himself. He didn't understand it. His entire life had been dictated by a schedule. Someone had always explained what would happen and when. He always knew what was expected of him, he always knew where he'd be at the end of the day.

None of this was true ever since he'd arrived on the Reservation yet right now, on horseback in a completely unfamiliar landscape led by a stranger who embodied a culture about which he knew nothing, he somehow felt it was right. He didn't know how this could be, but he did know one thing; he liked these people and he hoped they would grow to like and accept him.

The trail they followed was a reduction of the same road they had been on. The truck might have handled it for a mile or so without the trailer. But after that it narrowed and began to climb steeply. Lané reined in and allowed Zack to come alongside. He passed him a canteen.

Zack sipped, started to hand it back, but Lané put up a palm. "That one is yours. Keep it." He shifted slightly in his saddle, peering across the landscape. "To you, this land around us looks empty, I think, but there are people living out here." He pointed in several directions. "There, and over there, two families over that way." He was watching Zack's face. "My people are content to keep to themselves."

Zack stared across the barren tree studded landscape but saw nothing. It would be a long drive to the bank or grocery store from out here.

They rode up a shield of naked rock to the highest point yet and traversed a cliff edge then descended to another trail and followed it northwest at an easy ambling trot. A fence appeared, the first sign of humanity since they left the truck.

"We are here," Lané said. He dismounted, retrieving his rifle from its scabbard in the same motion. He led his horse with reins in one hand, rifle in the other. Zack followed him around a copse of tall oak trees. Before them was a small corral constructed from tree branches, twigs still attached. The corral was empty. The dung within was dry, there were no fresh disturbance in the dust. It had apparently not been used in many months. A trailer was directly behind the corral. Its shiny surface glimmered in the sun. It gave the appearance of disuse, overgrown with vegetation, dirt on the windows. Yet the door had a large, new-looking padlock.

Lané continued toward the trailer leading the black while Zack looped Babe's reins over the corral fence. He walked around behind the trailer. There was a large rear window with blinds closed on the inside. The remainder of the exterior was just as overgrown, just as dirty and projected disuse.

His walk brought him back to the door. Lané stood near the short metal steps leading up to it. He pointed to the ground where he stood. "People have been in and out of here a lot."

A profusion of boot prints led to and from the steps. There were prints from truck tires as well. Zack climbed the steps and took a close look at the lock. He saw tiny fresh scratches in the metal around the keyhole.

"Someone has used this lock recently," he said.

They studied the trailer, the cobwebs in the window apertures, the general look of disuse and decay.

"Maybe someone's storing stuff in there," Lané said.

"Seems the most likely thing," Zack said.

"Curtis is dead, the door is padlocked, but it feels to me like someone has just been here.

"There might be evidence in there to help us." Zack flipped the lock.

"There might. But I have no authority to break in. Do you?"

Zack shook his head. "I have even less authority than you at the moment. So what now?"

Lané glanced at the sun. "If we turn back now, we can sleep at home. "

That sounded good to Zack. But something gnawed at him. "Where are the sheep?"

"They are likely at a higher pasture."

Zack stood thinking. "We know someone has been here recently. Maybe there is another shepherd, someone who can give us more information." He jerked a thumb toward the trailer. "Maybe he can tell us what's in here."

"If we go look for the sheep, it will mean we camp out tonight."

Zack viewed the rising stone escarpment to the west and the sun just a hand span above it and sighed. "If we don't check now, we'll just have to come back another time, no doubt."

Lané grinned. "Let's go then. It is a long ride to the next motel." He chuckled to himself as he mounted the black.

They searched the ground west of the trailer and found prints and sheep droppings, shoe prints and shod horse prints. None looked fresh.

THE DARK ROAD

Lané pointed. "Last End Wash is that way. Sand Spring is the nearest water in the area. A shepherd would need to keep his sheep somewhere up there."

They rode into the sun, which had sunk enough to force them to lower their hat brims. The terrain was more rock than sand here and grew steeper with each half mile. They rode relaxed, enjoying the moment, their horses climbing the sandstone with ease.

Eventually, they came to a section that was long and steep. Lané dismounted. He gestured for Zack to do the same. "We have come to the ridge that forms the eastern wall of Last End Wash. We'll need to walk the horses from here. It gets steeper."

The climb was difficult. Sometime they followed wide cracks in the rock surface, sometimes they found a switch-back on an animal trail, sometimes there was sufficient soil to grip where trees clung to the slope. It was sweaty, hot work. Zack's clothing was soon soaked through. When at last they could go no higher and the ground began to slope away, they stopped. Zack immediately felt the chill of advancing evening in his wet clothing. He forgot his discomfort gazing at the view before him. Here was the entirety of Last End Wash—wide, desolate, serpentine sandstone along, sometimes rising like an inverted stream bed of bare rock, dry stream beds winding and worming their way along the wash.

Lané grinned. "Quite a view. It's all about erosion, the fast moving water cutting through the loose sandstone like a knife through butter. You can't tell from here, but some of those canyons are over one hundred feet deep. We'll keep to a trail that runs along this side until we get nearer the spring or until we find the sheep. Whichever comes first."

From where they stood, the descent into the wash seemed impossibly steep. "How will we get down there?" Zack asked.

Lané motioned off to their left. "There's a gulch over that way and a trail of sorts." He noticed Zack's uncertainty. "But not tonight. Tonight we'll camp up here."

Zack shivered. "Wouldn't it be warmer down there?"

The Navajo shook his head. "No, colder. Below us, up against the west facing cliff face, out of the sun most of the day, it stays pretty cold. There can be snow down there all summer some years. It wouldn't surprise me to find some tomorrow." He began to walk, leading Mystic down a slight slope toward a level area surrounded by trees. "We'll get a fire going and get warmed up," he said.

They set up a picket line for the horses, rubbed them down, fed them some grain from Lané's supply bag and left them to browse. Next in order was gathering old dry pinyon branches, which were in great supply. Soon the pyramid lean-to of wood crackled and moaned like a live thing. Out from Lané's magical bag came blankets. Using soft interwoven pine twigs they fashioned beds near the fire and lay the saddle blankets over them. Their saddles became pillows. When it was time to sleep, they would wrap themselves in the extra blankets Lané had brought.

The magic bag held a supply of nutrition bars and dried venison strips. Those, along with water, were their dinner and would be their breakfast too. They lounged by the bright warm fire as everything around them disappeared into blackness. The Navajo policeman was not much of a conversationalist, but Zack had enough questions burning inside him to keep the man talking regardless.

THE DARK ROAD

He learned Lané had been named Shorter not as a surname but because he was just that. He was the shorter of the two Begaye brothers and was called so by his community. He'd have preferred to be called Smarter, he said, grinning, because he figured he was but unfortunately it was Shorter that stuck.

"Where did Lané come from?"

"It is my called name. I was called Lané as a baby by my father for a favorite character in a book he was reading at the time. I always liked it." Lané studied Zack for a moment. "What do you know about clans?"

Zack shook his head, overwhelmed. "I tried to learn about them at the Navajo Museum, but it is all very strange. You are first known through your mother's clan, is that right?"

Lané nodded. "When I introduce myself to another Navajo I say Yá'át'ééh shí éí Lané Shorter Begaye yínishyé'. Next I introduce myself as born to The People Who Move About, my mother's clan, and born for the Red Bottom People, my father's clan. Sometimes I mention my grandparents' clans." He laughed. "After that, it is impossible to be a stranger." He looked at Zack. "Do you know that much about even your best friend?"

Zack shook his head. "I see what you mean."

Lané folded his hands behind his head on his saddle pillow. "Clans have an interesting history. There were only four created by Changing Woman in the beginning, now there are somewhere north of a hundred fifty, I've been told. Many came about from marriages into other Native American tribes, with Mexicans and even with whites." He rolled his eyes toward Zack. "Maybe someone in your history married a Navajo and started a clan. We could be related." He chuckled.

Zack smiled at the thought. "Maybe if we could think of the entire world population as one big clan, there'd be less strife."

"Oh, I don't know," Lané said. "There's plenty of strife among the clans." After a sleepy pause he said, "Always gonna be strife."

The night was still. Cold settled over them, held off only by the bubble of heat from the fire, now reduced to red winking coals. With his nose pinched by cold but his body warm in the blanket and the fire's heat, Zack was cozy. The nest of interwoven pine branches was comfortable and exuded a pleasant fragrance. The day had been arduous, and he was asleep before he could even think about it.

CHAPTER FOURTEEN

When Zack awoke it was still dark, although a slight rosiness to the eastern sky signaled its intentions. A man stood near the now cold ashes of the fire. Zack rose to his elbows. He knew this man.

It was the same Navajo, visible despite the dark, with long black braids and piercing dark eyes, the same flannel shirt and blue jeans tucked into scuffed boots, the white cowboy hat on his head. Again, the man stared not at Zack or anything near them but at something far beyond. He expressed the same anger and despair he had shown before. The specter was nearer this time, detail was more visible, and now Zack could see the crimson stain in the middle of the flannel shirt. The figure remained intent upon whatever it was he saw until once again he slowly faded away. When he was almost entirely gone, the entity became a small bright orb and like a shooting star flashed away into the wash below.

Zack was stunned.

"What did you see?" Lané's voice startled Zack.

"Did you see him too?"

Lané's eyes peeped out of his hoodie, his head still resting on the saddle. "I saw you lookin' like you saw something."

"He was just standing right there."

"Who?"

"The missing man, the dead man, Curtis Peaches." Zack described the apparition, the look on his face, his dress, and how he faded to an orb and flew down the canyon.

"Maybe he wants to show you something."

"Me? Why me?"

Lané moved up to a sitting position, his blanket wrapped around him like a teepee. "Damned if I know."

Zack too was sitting, shivering in the intruding cold. "Where does he want me to go?"

With a wave of his arm, Lané indicated the wash far below them. "Somewhere down there, if that's where his eyes were going, if that's where he went when he left."

Lané rose up now, his blanket discarded, and began to stack up twigs and unburnt wood to start a fire. After he had the kindling flaring, he turned away. "I'm gonna go pee, then I'll heat some water for breakfast."

"Don't feel much like breakfast," Zack mumbled through his blanket.

Lané turned his head back toward him and laughed. "No worries there, we don't got much anyhow." He headed off into the trees, still chuckling.

Zack opened his blanket to welcome the fire's warmth as the flame built from the kindling and scaled the wood itself. His senses had been overpowered the first time he'd seen the apparition. Never before in his life had he experienced such a thing, not outside of dreams or movies, anyway. He'd put it aside the first time as best he could, telling himself it was a manifestation of the anxiety and worries of culture shock, not to speak of the excitement of being out with a pretty and very exotic young woman at the time.

There was no way to ignore it now. The Navajo man had looked as real as Lané looked right now returning from the trees. Every detail of the apparition's features, clothing, manner had been just as real. Yet he wasn't, he couldn't be.

"He wasn't real," Zack said, saying it aloud for his own benefit.

"Maybe he was a *hozoji*. They are in harmony with the supernatural powers, the Holy People. A *hozoji* stands in two worlds."

"But why me? Why did he come to me?"

Lané looked at him for a moment, mumbled to himself as he dug into his satchel. "You are the only white man I know who has seen the *hozoji*. I did not know such a thing could happen. It must mean there is something for you to do, something only you can do."

From the depths of his magic bag came a tin pot. Once the lid was removed, he extracted two tin cups, one of which he handed to Zack, and several paper packets he set aside. He filled the pot with water from the large canteen and set it on the coals, then went to care for the horses.

Zack sat on his bed, his blanket around him and stared at the water in the tin pot. There was so much new in his life now, so many unexpected, unbelievable things to consider. Once the water boiled he found the instant coffee, put some in each cup and took a steaming cup to Lané.

The approach to the ravine where it slashed its way to the wash below was steep, the rock filled ravine itself even rougher. They stayed mounted this time, the horses picked their way along a track worn among the rocks by many creatures traveling this way over the years, including herds of sheep, no doubt. At times the incline was such Zack thought he might fall forward over his horse's neck. Lané leaned back on the big black and seemed to flow as part of his horse.

Where the ravine opened into the wideness of a dry flow in the wash basin, Zack saw that Lané had been right about the cold here. There was indeed snow, tucked up against the base of the cliff, two or three inches deep, crystalized into ice around the edges—in July!

Now the ride was easy, the dry stream bed flat and sandy, nothing to avoid but the occasional creosote bush or smoke tree cluster waiting for the next cloudburst to replenish their water supply. They rode south, the sun creeping across Zack's left shoulder to project a shadow cartoon of a man on horseback. The streambed narrowed, the sides steepened and grew until the men rode in a roofless tunnel deeper into the vastness of the wash.

Lané cast thoughtful glances over his shoulder at the sky. "Weather looks good," he said. "But if a rainstorm happens up toward Navajo Mountain we could be in trouble here."

"You mean a flash flood?"

Lané nodded. "This cut narrows and gets deeper before we climb out. We just have to keep an ear out."

"Ear?"

"Yeah, we'll hear it before we see it and by then it's too late anyway, probably."

Zack looked at the canyon walls. Nowhere to go. "So why come this way?"

Lané shrugged. "It's just a short bit, but it saves hours of riding time."

"Do the sheep come down here?"

"No. They just mosey and eat their way along the surface of the wash. They're in no hurry."

"Shouldn't we be up there looking for them?"

Lané reined in, let Zack come alongside. "Two things. First, they need the water at Sand Spring, which is down that way." He pointed ahead. "Second, where we come out if they been through there we'll cut their trail. If not, we go back north the slow way and look for 'em." He glanced back over his shoulder again. "No clouds up north. I think we're good."

As the canyon walls mounted, Zack imagined a sudden rush of water in these narrow confines. As remote as the possibility was, it painted a nerve-wracking picture. The canyon heights grew to seem unassailable. Then Lané gave Mystic a nudge to the left, heading toward a place in the wall that grew to a defile as they neared and opened into a narrow passage just wide enough for the horsemen to ride single file. It wound like a snake in a gradual ascent until they were once again up in the wideness of the huge wash basin.

Zack looked back over his shoulder for a view of the deep canyon they had just left but could see no sign of it. The wide brush studded wash just seemed to sweep uninterrupted to the next set of cliffs. Ahead of them, the full width of the wash narrowed funnel-like, contained by towering dam-like cliffs.

"There's a spring up there," Lané said, "just beneath that high cliff wall. Probably where the water gathers when the floods come. There's no place for it to run off, so it pools and sinks into the sands. You can find water there most times of the year if you dig a bit."

As he spoke, the Navajo leaned low in his saddle, inspecting the ground. Before long he sat upright with a grin. "There they are," he said, pointing. "Sheep. The tracks look recent, too. Now all we got to do is follow them."

They did, while the sun brightened and burned and the cliffs loomed larger. The sheep trail meandered on down the wash, working south. Zack saw other hoof prints, sometimes boot prints, sometimes the prints of a large dog working along the herd.

They came to a place where the ground sloped steeply away before them. They looked down at a stream bed which actually held water creating a muddy path along its course. The sheep tracks scurried down the slope toward it. Near a bend in the narrow course, just upstream, was a wooden corral. Beyond it were clear sets of tire prints circling near the corral and then off into the distance of the upper wash.

"I guess we know what happened to the sheep," Lané said. "Someone loaded them up and trucked them off."

"Let's ride down there and see if we can learn anything else," Zack said.

Their mounts handle the slope easily. Lané was able to read the signs. Two men and a dog had gathered the sheep herd and trucked them away. There was nothing more to see.

"Let's ride to the spring," Lané said. "We can water the horses and cool down for our return trip." He led off and Zack followed.

The landscape was in a word monumental with high rising walls all around them. They approached Sand Spring along the bed of the creek, where occasional muddy puddles still glistened in the sun. The horses' hooves kicked up mud as they rode.

The spring was located where the narrow wash was forced into a large bend by towering sandstone walls. Here they found several deeper pools for the horses to water. The men dismounted, stretched their legs and had some lunch. Zack found a dry stone to sit on and gazed up at the cliff face as he ate, admiring the variety of colors produced by the play of light and shadow. The sky above it was pure blue.

One particular shadow caught his eye. It was a vertical crack up the face of the sandstone on the side where the wash began its bend. Loose red stone piled at its base looked as if it had fallen recently. Curious, Zack stood and ambled over toward it, munching his nutrition bar.

He inspected the crack. It was about six inches wide at the bottom. Some recent force, perhaps a flood or a trembler had widened it enough to loosen chunks of stone high up. He picked up one of them. It was of red clay, regular at its corners as if it had been fashioned by hand, not nature.

Straining his neck he could see where the crack widened substantially. He saw similar stone chunks edging out of the darkness of the larger crack. His curiosity overwhelmed him and Zack wedged his feet into the small crack and began to climb. He found firm nooks to support his hands and feet. When his eyes reached the level where the crack widened he gazed in amazement. Before him was a clay brick wall, beyond it rose an entire city, or so it appeared in the half light.

"What do you see?" Lané called from below.

"I think it is the ruin of a cliff dwelling," Zack said. His response was a half whisper affected by an overwhelming feeling he might disturb spirits in this ancient place.

"You should go no farther. There are harmful spirits in these places."

Zack studied the sides of the wider crack, saw where some carved nooks were placed along the void until they reached the large stone shelf the structures were built upon. Whoever his predecessors were, they had gone on.

"I'm going in," he told Lané. Without waiting for a reply, Zack grasped the edge of the crack and placed a shoe onto a foothold. He found more handholds to support his climb and eventually he stepped onto the shelf.

There was more light inside the cave than he expected, apparently coming from a crack leading to the surface. A huge shift of the earth at some recent time had exposed this ancient cliff dwelling. The original access, he saw now, would have been by a narrow opening high on the cliff face, from there probably hand and toe holds to the top. Fearing some formidable foe, these people had constructed their homes in a large hidden cavern.

He stepped carefully among a small community of a dozen or so houses and smaller buildings, probably storage units. Everything was remarkably well kept, the walls virtually untouched, wooden roof beams in place, roofs and ceilings solid. The dust of the ages covered everything.

He saw fresh foot prints in the dust, boots, and sandals. Other people had made this discovery. He followed the prints into a room, ducking through the small doorway. Inside it was dark, but his eyes adjusted enough to see outlines in the dust where objects had once been but were now gone. Round imprints suggested pottery, or baskets, other dust outlines must have been various tools or personal objects. Earthen shelves that once held treasures were emptied.

Zack followed footprints from room to dusty room. Every one was the same. There had been artifacts in all of them until very recently—now they were gone.

CHAPTER FIFTEEN

Zack scrambled back to the cave opening. Lané stood below, looking up.

"You should see this!" Zack said.

"I will not go up there. I do not wish to leave footprints for some spirit from another world to follow me."

"You are missing quite a sight." He climbed down, finding the descent much more difficult. Once down, he washed his hands at the spring. Lané stood near holding both horses.

Zack glanced up at him. "That's an amazingly well preserved ruin. I think there were intact artifacts in there until very recently."

"Maybe the truck picked up more than sheep," Lané said.

Zack nodded. "That's what I was thinking." He stood and glanced around at the ground. "I don't see any truck tire imprints here, just sheep and horses. Whoever robbed this place did not want to leave evidence of their crime."

"You think they transported it all by hand?"

"That's what I think. They lowered the pieces by rope and hand carried them up to the corral," Zack said.

Lané whistled. "That would take many hours and much hard work."

"Do you remember the truck tire prints back at the trailer?" Zack asked.

"Yes."

"Let's take another look those tire prints at the sheep corral."

The two men rode back along the stream bed the way they had come. At the corral, Lané swung down and went to where the truck had parked. It didn't take him long. "I know there are many trucks with tires like this, but these are the same."

Zack leaned forward over his pommel, watching. "Measure the width. We can check to see if the tire size is the same when we return to the trailer."

At that moment the packed sand directly in front of Lané's hand erupted into a fountain of dust. The sound of the shot came milliseconds later, reverberating off the massive cliff faces like a doomsday warning. Lané reacted instantly. He leapt up behind his horse and removed the rifle from its scabbard in a single fluid motion.

Zack had already tumbled off his horse, the reins still in his hand. "Where did that come from?" he asked.

"Not sure," Lané said. "But I think up there on the ridge where we came down." He supported his rifle across his saddle as he searched the skyline.

They waited. The shot was not repeated.

"We will need to find another way home," Lané said.

Zack took out his phone but was not surprised there was no service. "Do you know another way?"

"There are many ways. But right now we need to get into a better position. We'll walk away from here leading the horses, keeping the horse between you and that ridgeline behind us."

Slowly, carefully Zack took the mare's reins in his right hand and held his rifle in his left. The men followed the truck tracks north. They were in wide open ground, completely exposed.

"Why don't we go in toward the base of the ridge? We're pretty vulnerable out here," Zack said.

Lané constantly surveyed the land around them. "He will be expecting that and be waiting for us. I think he's not a good shot or I'd be dead. We'll make him try to shoot us at long range out here. Up ahead at that slight bend there are large pine trees. When we get there, we'll move in among them."

Zack frowned. "Won't he be there waiting for us?"

"No. Where he must travel is more difficult and will take him longer. We should be among the trees before he gets there. We can turn the tables on him."

It was after midday and it was very hot. Sweat ran down Zack's spine. Despite Lané's confidence he imagined the thwunck of a bullet into his horse or some part of himself at any moment.

It took twenty minutes to reach the pines. Each minute felt like an hour to Zack, particularly as they neared the trees. If the shooter was lurking there, they would be at his mercy.

Apparently, he wasn't. In the trees Lané led the way to a trail of sorts near the escarpment base. For the first time Zack felt somewhat safe.

At a water break, Lané explained his plan. "We can cross this ridge farther up the wash than he would expect. From there we can take a different road to reach my rig."

"But what about the trailer?" Zack asked.

"The trailer?"

"The trailer with the lock on it. We need to go there."

"Why?"

"I will bet that's where the artifacts are stashed," Zack said.

Lané stared at Zack. "Yes, and I am pretty sure that is where the shooter will go. He expects us to go there."

"Then we agree. We can capture the killer and recover the artifacts all at the same time."

Lané shook his head, looked away for a while, then back at Zack. "You are one crazy white man. But, okay, we will try."

Zack grinned. "We'll think of a plan."

Lané studied the wall of rising stone beside them. "If we do that we must cross this ridge sooner." In a moment he nodded to himself as if satisfied and turned his horse around. "We need to go back a short distance, but I think there is a way. He will not expect us there, but we might stumble onto him. We must make no noise and be always on the alert."

They rode back along the escarpment out of the trees but remained tight to the cliff base. Another ten minutes and the sheer rock gave way to an opening, a narrow crack with tumbled rocks partially blocking it.

Lané dismounted and led his horse in among the boulders, picking his way. Zack followed right behind.

It was difficult, steep, sometimes it meant scrambling over precipitous rock with exposure to falls that could mean severe injury if not death to man or horse. The two men did not speak; the only sounds were the scattering of small stones, the clatter of hoofs across rock and heavy breathing from men and beasts.

When at last they emerged from the narrow confines of the slot, they stepped into the warmth of the sun which was welcome after the cold of the deep and narrow ravine. They were in a stand of tall pines. To the left the escarpment rose even higher, but before them the ground sloped downward toward the flats. They mounted and rode down at a walk, continually on the alert. Lané's rifle lay across the saddle before him, Zack kept his pistol ready.

Although they crossed roads that would have made travel easier, Lané avoided them. He kept to untraveled places in the lee of mounds of rock or brush. Always their eyes scanned the open spaces, they held still at trees and brush cover until sure it was clear. After an hour of riding Lané motioned to Zack to wait and urged the black up a steep rock face. In minutes, he reappeared. His cell phone was in his hand, and he smiled. He'd found a signal and called for help. Zack felt much better.

They continued at a slow walk trying not to raise dust. An occasional breeze swept over Zack's wet face and felt good. Their next stop was behind a small stand of pines.

Lané leaned in and spoke softly to Zack. "Beyond these trees is a rock outcropping. Beyond that is the trailer. The shooter will likely be in those rocks waiting for us to come down the road we took on our way out. That road is beyond the trailer to the northwest." He indicated with a cutting motion. "We must wait for the signal to tell us help has arrived. After that, I need you to ride along this side of this rock outcrop. You will come to an open area. The trailer will be just beyond. There are several large pines, large enough for cover. Ride to them. If the shooter sees you in the open area he will wait for me to appear before firing. He will want to know where I am. Once you reach the trees stay in their cover and wait. Do not continue toward the trailer. Just stay there." He studied Zack's face. "Did you get all that?"

Zack nodded.

They waited, the horses occasionally snuffled and shifted. They were in shade and the breeze was comfortable. An hour went by. Neither spoke.

When Lané's phone made a short bird-like chirp, he looked at Zack and nodded. Zack followed his instructions, stayed

115

close to the base of the rock which rose somewhere high up beyond his sight. He rounded a corner and saw the trailer. No one was there that he could see. No truck, no horses. Looking to the right he saw the small group of trees Lané had mentioned, but between them and him was a very large open space.

Zack took a deep breath and urged the mare forward. Although Lané's logic was sound, he had no faith the killer wouldn't shoot. He had never felt so completely vulnerable. He made himself ride at an easy walk as if he had no suspicions of an ambush, but when he reached the cover of the pine grove he gave a great sigh of relief.

Now came the wait.

Zack dismounted and tied Babe's reins loosely to a tree branch. If a gunfight erupted, he did not wish to endanger her. He didn't know what would happen next, but he supposed Lané's signal meant other native police were in the area and perhaps would be able to draw the shooter from the rocks. All he could do was wait.

He didn't have to wait long. A figure appeared in front of him in the open ground. Zack drew his pistol then held it half raised in front of him. The man's features became more distinct. It was not the killer, it was the apparition, Curtis Peaches—flannel shirt with bloodstained front, blue jeans tucked into boots, white hat, same expression as before. But now the spirit's focus seemed less distant, focused on something behind Zack.

Zack turned slowly, keeping his gun shielded by his body and the rear of the horse. A man stood fifty feet away where he'd stepped out from behind a tree. He had a rifle and it was leveled at Zack. He wore an army camouflaged shirt and pants. He was shorter than average with broad features, a Native American.

116

"Where is the other one?" the man asked in a low, husky voice.

Zack shook his head. "I don't know. He didn't tell me where he would go."

The man stared at Zack. His rifle never wavered.

"What did he tell you to do?"

"Wait. Just wait."

"Keep the white man safe, is that it? The brandy-new FBI agent? Oh, yes, I know about you. Well, Mr. FBI, you are going to have a short career." His body tensed. Zack knew the talk was over.

A loud bird chirp sounded close by. It distracted the man for a millisecond, his rifle wavered and Zack raised his pistol and fired. As the gun bucked in his hand he heard the sound of a rifle, saw a lick of flame. I'm too late, he thought. The man crumpled to the ground, his rifle drooped from his hands, and he lay still. Zack became aware of another figure near the tree, another rifle pointed at the man. Holding that rifle was Eagle Feather.

A minute later, Jimmy Chaparral appeared followed by two Navajo policemen. As Jimmy kicked the rifle away, one of the policemen put fingers at the man's neck, feeling for a pulse. Eagle Feather kept his rifle trained on him the entire time. Only when the policeman slowly shook his head did Eagle Feather relax and let the barrel droop.

Zack watched it all as if from a different place. He was surprised not to feel shock. He knew he wasn't hit, the man's shot had missed. He put his pistol away and walked to the gathering policemen.

Eagle Feather nodded to Zack. "Nice shooting, White Man."

Zack shook his head. "I was too slow."

Lané arrived from the rocks. He looked at Zack, saw he was unhurt. "It did not quite work out as planned, did it?"

Jimmy looked at Lané. "The man guessed your move and managed to isolate Zack. I reckon he planned to come for you after that. He didn't figure on the rest of us."

Lané gave a wry grin. "No one ever thinks you can get a cell signal out here.

Jimmy gave the body a nudge, leaned down, and stared into his face. "Anybody recognize this guy?"

All the Navajos shook their heads.

Lané searched the man's pockets, came up with another rifle magazine, a wallet, a set of keys, which he tossed to Jimmy.

Jimmy reached for the wallet. There was no ID—just a few loose bills. "He's too clean. Probably a pro. We're gonna need help on this one." He got on his cell phone. "Lenana, we need a meat wagon up here, a forensics unit, and a team for a cop related shooting. You may need help from Tuba City on this one. Oh, and call Ben Brewster and tell him his rookie recruit was involved in a shooting."

No one said anything after Jimmy put his phone away, but in the silence that followed Zack felt a wave of new respect.

"I think it's time we looked inside the trailer," Sergeant Chaparral said.

CHAPTER SIXTEEN

Jimmy, Lané, and Zack walked slowly toward the trailer. They stared at the huge lock for a moment. Jimmy studied the dead man's key ring, found the Yale key and opened the door.

It was dark inside. Lané flipped up the window shades and a view of the interior was revealed. They stared in astonishment. Half of the trailer was stuffed from floor to ceiling with taped up boxes. An eight foot folding table was up against the wall. Both the table and the floor under it were covered with artifacts—bowls, pitchers, seashell jewelry, baskets, ceramic ladles, pots, mortars and pestles, various wooden tools, woven reed animals, painted gourds, woven sandals—the list went on. There was packaging tape in a dispenser, plastic wrap on a large roll, a huge stack of newspapers.

Lané glanced at Zack. "You think all this came from that one site you found?"

Zack shook his head. "They must have found some other untouched ruins to have this much stuff."

"Look at all those boxes." Lané looked at the stack nearest him. "These boxes are ready to be shipped. There's no address label, but they must have someone willing to deal in stolen goods."

Jimmy was studying a ledger. "These men were collecting a lot of money from this business. This ledger shows items ordered and amounts for individual pieces. We're talking three and four figures for some of it." He flipped pages. "Real cagey, no names or addresses listed anywhere." He glanced at the boxes. "See, no return address, just blank boxes. Take 'em to any UPS office and handle everything else by computer."

Jimmy, Lané, and Zack made a thorough search of the trailer but found nothing helpful. The place was being used strictly to receive the artifacts and pack them for shipping. A truck would then drive here and back up to the door. They would load it and then take the boxes to whichever UPS outlet they decided upon or maybe even use several.

The men stepped out into the sunshine, it felt cool compared to the stifling trailer. Jimmy turned to a nearby officer. "Get a crime scene lock on this door and plaster the place with yellow tape, please."

Lané was kneeling near a truck track, measuring it with his hand. "Same size tire," he said, looking up at Zack.

Zack turned to Jimmy. "You'll want to get someone out to Last End Wash to take a photo of the tire tracks out there. If you can match them to these, there's a chain of evidence for you."

Jimmy nodded.

Zack looked around. "Where's Eagle Feather? The man just saved my life."

Jimmy smiled. "He's gone to borrow Big Blue so they can backtrack this guy and prove he was the one who took the shot at Lané. They can also prove whether he was in or around the pilfered ruin." He scanned the distant clumps of trees. "Now we got to find a vehicle."

"What vehicle?"

Jimmy smiled. "I don't think our man walked out here from Shonto." He gave instructions to a policeman to search the area. "Better take these." Jimmy tossed him the car keys. Then he pulled out his phone. "I'm gonna call the Antiquities people to come get their stuff," he told Zack and Lané and walked away, waving a backward hand.

Lané grinned at Zack. "Let's mount up, get to the trailer, get these horses home and find ourselves a big dinner."

Zack liked that idea.

Later in the truck, Zack told Lané about the latest manifestation Curtis Peaches had made and how it warned him he was in danger.

Lané didn't respond for a while, staring ahead as he drove. The trailer occasionally creaked and groaned but the highway was smooth. Zack heard little from the horses, they were probably sleeping. The roadside sage appeared double in size with their long shadows cast by a sinking sun.

"I have said, and I say it again. He has chosen you for some purpose. It will unfold with time."

The big dinner the men dreamt about never came to be. Zack was called to appear before Ben Brewster who reviewed the formalities involved in an agent shooting.

"This one is a bit more complicated because it happened on the Reservation. The FBI will want it kept as quiet as possible so as not to stir up feelings. But from what I understand, it was Eagle Feather who fired the fatal shot. Anyway, not my job to question you. A team will come up from Flagstaff for that." Brewster gave Zack a reassuring look. "Don't worry too much. You were in a clearly defensive situation. However, I will need your weapon for ballistic testing." He accepted Zack's pistol and pushed another Glock 19M across the desk. "Use this one in the meantime. You should carry on with Sergeant Chaparral, close down this antiquities theft ring."

Zack felt exonerated. Although he knew the FBI Shooting Team experience might be far more intensive, he was relieved by Ben's reassurance.

Bella looked up as he emerged from the inner sanctum. "Still in one piece, I see."

Zack spread his arms to show he had all his parts. "I am."

She gave a small pout. "Then you have no reason not to ask me out or would you rather be out camping with the boys?"

"Dinner?"

"I'm off at five. I'll meet you at the Quality Inn at six."

Zack stepped out into the dusty street feeling happy and relieved. He also felt very tired. The day had been arduous, the experience intensely emotional, and his anxiety over the shooting still hung about him. He hoped he wouldn't fall asleep over dinner with Bella. He probably should have said no, but he was really glad of the company.

When he walked past the reception area on his way to the elevator he saw a slender figure extricate himself from a chair like a bad dream. Jimmy Chaparral met him in front of the reception desk.

"Let's take a walk," he said.

Zack turned without a word and walked with him out into the dusk.

"We've learned a lot since you left. It's important we share now, before we go."

"We go?" Zack's heart sank.

"You'll see." They leaned against a rail near the motel entrance. "We've learned the shooter's identity."

Zack became alert.

"His name is Kenneth Nez."

Zack didn't recognize the name. He gave Jimmy a questioning look.

"You shot Ashkii Nez's son."

Zack was staggered. "Ashkii's son?" His memory took him back to the framed photograph on the mantel in Ashkii's hogan, the woman and little boy. He'd shot the man's son.

Jimmy gave him a moment to digest the information. "We located Kenneth Nez's car, a Subaru. We're going over it. There was some dope and a pistol in the glove compartment. The interior was a mess, like he'd been sleeping in it a number of times. Also a lot of dog hair. And we found this." Jimmy handed Zack a spent rifle cartridge. "It's a Remington .223, same gauge forensics says was likely used to kill Peaches. It was just lying under the driver seat."

Zack was stunned. Had they actually found the man who killed Curtis Peaches?

Jimmy was watching his face. "There is still a lot to be done. Ken's car will need a complete forensic going over. We're looking for prints or DNA from Curtis Peaches in it. We need to have forensics tell us what breed of dog left that hair and those prints. Eagle Feather is still out there trying to connect Kenneth to the ancient ruin and the man who shot at Lané." Jimmy grinned. "Still a lot of questions, but today we sure got a lot of answers."

"Not happy ones for Ashkii," Zack said.

"Nope." He stood, straightened his jacket. "We know what we gotta do. You ready?"

"Let's go."

Zack left a message at the front desk for Bella. They climbed into Jimmy's Bronco and headed east out of town. It was dark now, the headlights were twin tunnels of brightness that reduced the huge landscape around them to a tiny world of lighted brush flashing by and flickering moths that came and went.

They rode silently, Zack going over in his mind how to tell a man his son was dead and that he, Zack, was the one who had shot him, this to a man who had offered him hospitality and kindness his first night in this land without hesitation. It didn't matter what the boy had done, a parent is a parent.

Jimmy interrupted his thoughts. "We never found the computer."

"Computer?"

"Yeah, we figured whoever was keeping the books for that operation had to be doing it on a computer, maybe a laptop, iPad, something portable."

"Makes sense."

"It wasn't in the trailer, it wasn't in Kenneth's car."

"Did Kenneth have a home, an apartment?"

"Turns out he's a fugitive from the Army. He couldn't show his face around town too much, so I doubt he had digs in town."

"He would need internet, so he couldn't keep it in a cave somewhere," Zack said.

"Right."

"Suppose we say Curtis Peaches was Kenneth's partner— we know he couldn't have done all that by himself. Couldn't he be keeping the computer?" Zack asked.

"I think Morning Flower would have given it to us, if only to help find Curtis, if he had one. It wasn't among Curtis' things. And don't forget, Curtis had been living the shepherd life out at Last End Wash so a computer would have been little use to him there."

Zack was silent.

Jimmy said, "We find the computer, we find all the evidence."

They were driving the dirt road down into the canyon where Ashkii lived.

"I don't see any lights down there. Last time we came he had a light at the sheep pen and light from the window," Jimmy said.

"Maybe he's not home?"

Jimmy grunted. He drove up to within a hundred yards of the hogan and stopped, turned off the engine, left the headlights glowing on the side of the hogan. Through the open window they could hear sheep—lots of sheep.

"He's got more sheep than the last time we came," Jimmy said.

They waited five minutes.

As if by signal both men opened their doors and stepped out, silently closing them. Jimmy left the headlights on. The scent of sage and smell of sheep mingled together. Near at hand a cricket sounded. No lights came on, no one appeared in the headlights, nothing happened. They walked around toward the east facing front door, groping their way, letting their eyes adjust to the dark. The mewling and baaing told them the sheep were corralled near the pen. It had to be a large flock.

"Could be those sheep are the group from Last End Wash," Jimmy whispered

When they arrived at the thick front door, Jimmy knocked loudly and announced himself.

There was no response.

He repeated himself, louder this time and followed it with three loud knocks. He looked at Zack. "I think we better go in. He could be hurt or ill."

Zack's nodded and Jimmy tried the door handle. The latch shifted, the door swung open. Immediately something sprung out of the darkness and smashed into Jimmy. The weight and impact knocked both men back out the door and slammed Jimmy on his back. A large animal stood on his chest, it's head at his face. Zack saw it turn toward him. Before he could react it was on him, a long warm tongue sloshing across his face. It was a very large dog and it was delighted to see them.

Zack rubbed it behind the ears and managed to push it aside sufficiently to stand.

Jimmy was laughing. "Scared the shit out of me," he said. He was standing now, brushing the dust from his pants.

"I think it's an Old English Sheep Dog," Zack said. He looked at its huge paws. "I think that explains those mysterious paw prints we've been finding."

"I think it explains what happened to Curtis Peaches the night he was abducted. He was attacked, all right, by a hundred fifty pounds of loving dog."

"That's how the killer got him into the car so easily. He was meeting two old friends," Zack said.

Jimmy held up a finger, seemed to sense something. He swung his head, searching. "The question is, what is this dog doing here?"

As if in answer to his question they heard the simultaneous report of a rifle and a thunk of a bullet hitting the house. Both men went to the ground and crawled to cover.

"Ashkii? Ashkii Nez? Is that you? It's Jimmy Chaparral. I've come to see you."

Another bullet ploughed through sand near Jimmy's head. "Shit!" Jimmy yelled and rolled away.

Zack tried to slither away in the opposite direction. A bullet slammed into the stucco just above his head. He decided to make himself one with the earth.

"White man, you killed my son." It was Ashkii's voice.

"Ashkii, don't do this," Jimmy yelled. "It wasn't him. We need to talk." He shouted some other words in Navajo.

Another shot, another bullet, this time skinning the ground near Jimmy.

"He's not buying it," Jimmy mumbled. He called to Zack. "We can't stay here. I'm going to make a run for the corner of the building. He doesn't want to kill me, he wants to kill you. After I draw his attention, then you go for it."

Zack saw the shadowy figure rise and run. He heard the shot, scrambled up and ran, diving around the corner. Another shot sounded and bits of wood debris hit his face, but he was behind the corner of the house and safe. He crept on around the building until he saw another figure. "Jimmy?"

"Yeah."

"You okay?" Zack moved to him. They sat together side by side, backs against the building.

"Plan A went south, what's plan B?" Zack asked.

"I've been trying to figure out where he is. Maybe over by the shed. I don't want to shoot the old guy."

"Well he sure wants to shoot me," Zack said.

"Yeah. I think plan B involves keeping you out of it." He took out his phone, made a call. "Lenana, the old boy is giving us resistance. Send out the nearest guys with flashing lights, would you?" He listened to her question. "Yeah, we're all fine so far." Jimmy put the phone away. "It will be at least ten minutes until the nearest car can get here." He paused, sighed. "So here's the plan. You stay right here, just watch for movement in case he comes looking for you. I'm going to go find him."

Without another word, Jimmy was gone.

Zack did as he was told and stayed put. His gaze swept slowly across the visible landscape watching for even the slightest movement. He wondered where the dog was, then figured it must be with the sheep doing its job or with its owner, if indeed Ashkii was its owner. Zack had worked up a sweat, the night was growing cold. He felt chilled just sitting here, but he could not afford any movement. If Ashkii was near here and Zack made any move, it would be over. He thought about how ridiculous this was, two skilled Navajo Indians slithering through the underbrush and the novice FBI target sitting here waiting to be shot. A month ago, such a situation would not have occurred to him, not in his wildest dreams. He wanted to look at his watch but didn't dare. How long could ten minutes be, anyway.

Then he heard a shout. He couldn't make out the words, but he knew it wasn't Jimmy. It was Ashkii. Zack crept low around the building toward the sound of the voice. Rounding a corner, he saw a light. The shed light had been turned on. It shone down on the fence where the sheep huddled just beyond. On the near side of the fence stood Ashkii. In front of him facing the other way knelt Jimmy. Ashkii held his rifle barrel against his head.

"FBI man, come here to me or I will shoot Jimmy and then I will come find you anyway."

CHAPTER SEVENTEEN

Jimmy's voice came to him but muffled, words unintelligible. Zack realized he was gagged, his hands probably tied behind him. Would the old Navajo shoot another Navajo, an acquaintance to whom he had offered hospitality just the other night, a respected policeman? Zack's short studies of the culture didn't begin to help with this situation. He had no idea what Ashkii would do.

Zack rose slowly, put his pistol on the ground, put his hands in the air.

"Walk toward me," Ashkii said.

Zack began to walk, a step, another step, another.

"Keep coming. I want to see the face of the man who killed my son as he dies."

Zack stayed put. Not much incentive in that.

"I will count to five and then I will shoot this man unless you step closer. One. Two. Three..."

Oh, shit, Zack thought. Does it matter if he shoots me here or there? "Okay, okay, here I come." Zack took a step, then launched himself toward Ashkii. He would never make it, he knew that. It was just too far. But it was better than dying without trying.

Ashkii's rifle moved up from behind Jimmy's neck and Zack saw it pointed directly at him. He wondered how it would feel as the bullet entered his brain or maybe he wouldn't feel it at all. The rifle barrel looked huge, the opening where the bullet would emerge like an enormous tunnel.

Then the impossible happened. What Zack thought at first was a large sheep rose up next to the fence and snatched Ashkii's rifle away.

Zack's rush had taken him as far as Jimmy. He stumbled and fell to his knees, gaping up at the scene before him. The sheep he had seen fell from the man's back where it had unwillingly ridden and scurried off complaining loudly and now Eagle Feather stood with Ashkii's rifle turned back on its owner. Ashkii could only stare.

"Why don't you go get your gun and take this man into custody, White Man?" Eagle Feather said. "I see you forgot it next to the house."

Zack somehow rose to his feet, his legs trembling beneath him, and walked back, picked up his gun and returned. He held the pistol on Ashkii as Eagle Feather climbed over the fence. He then ordered Ashkii to a prone position and zip-tied his hands behind his back. Eagle Feather was untying Jimmy and chuckling.

"I'm sure you had a plan," he said to his friend.

"Of course, I did, but you came along and spoiled it," Jimmy said.

I thought you had gone with the tracker dog to Last End Wash," Zack said to Eagle Feather.

"I didn't go out there with Big Blue. I asked Libby Whittaker, the trainer, to track Kenneth. She's the better handler. When I got back to Elk Springs, I looked for Jimmy. Lenana told me he planned to go see Ashkii Nez and tell him the news of his son. So, I came here."

"I'm sure glad you did," Zack said.

They walked Ashkii into his hogan and made him comfortable. He told them where to find the coffee and all that they needed to make it. By now the patrol car had shown up with two Navajo policemen and all six people sat around the room and had coffee and fry bread. Now that it was all over, Ashkii was the most amiable of hosts.

"The white man did not kill your son," Eagle Feather told Ashkii. "Kenneth had tried to shoot Lané to stop them from reporting the discovery of the Anasazi ruin, which would lead to their crime. He missed. He decided to wait and ambush them when they returned to the trailer. He caught the FBI man from behind, held his rifle on him. The white man had his gun out but not raised. He tried to raise the gun to defend himself but was too slow." Eagle Feather looked at Zack. "That seems to happen to you a lot." He shrugged. "So I shot Kenneth. I shot him before he could shoot the FBI agent. That is what happened."

The room was quiet after that, just the sipping of coffee.

Ashkii spoke. "This is a sad day, but I am glad I have not killed the white man." He looked down, his eyes closed momentarily, then looked up again, chin raised, pride showing in his face. "I will tell you the story of how all this came to be."

Ashkii began to speak in Navajo. Jimmy translated for Zack.

"I think it best to start the story at the beginning," Ashkii said. "There was a man who owned a flock of sheep. The sheep fed and clothed his family and the man took occasional part-time jobs. His father had kept sheep, so this man continued in the tradition. But where he lived, forage was almost gone and he could not afford to buy feed so he looked for better pasturage. He found it in the Sand Spring area of Last End Wash. No one else was there or wanted it. He moved his sheep up there. It was good. The herd grew. The man purchased a dog to help him so that he

131

could be with his family for short visits. Still, he had to be away from them for long periods of time. His wife grew tired of this arrangement and left him. His son grew up without fatherly advice and guidance and became wild and unruly. At his father's suggestion, and to get away from poverty, his son joined the army and entered an elite fighting group. He did well there, but his continued opposition to authority gave him many problems. One day he went too far and to avoid prison, he and a comrade deserted."

Ashkii paused to sip some water a policeman had given him.

"The deserters ran and tried to find a place to hide. The man's son brought his friend to where his father kept his flock at Last End Wash, a place where no one ever goes. His father was surprised to see him. He was not happy about the reasons, but loved his son and was glad to have him back. He agreed to let the two deserters stay and care for the sheep, and the father would take a few sheep home with him and tend them there. In that way no one would need to go to Last End Wash, even if they needed to see the father.

"They did this and for a while the plan worked well. No one ever went to Dead End Wash or thought to look for them there. Then one day the son's comrade found an unknown Anasazi ruin while climbing the rock walls of the canyon. They explored it. It was untouched, full of artifacts. They knew the worth of this discovery. They began to collect pieces in the utility trailer. One day the father discovered the collection and confronted them. He was very unhappy with them but when they told him the worth of the artifacts, this man, who had known poverty all his life, changed his mind.

THE DARK ROAD

"The road of life stretches out before every human being. The road has many divides. At these divides every human being must choose the light road or the dark road. Sometimes it is hard to see the dark road. It is like Coyote and plays tricks on human beings. When the man saw how much money they could make from the artifacts, he chose the dark road.

"The man asked where they could sell these artifacts without getting caught. The son and his friend found the answer on the internet, the dark net, they called it. There was a dealer in Flagstaff experienced in such transactions who would purchase the pieces. They bought a truck and drove the artifacts to him and he paid them in cash. There would be no records of these transactions. They did not deposit the money in a bank but hid it and spent it carefully. Once all the artifacts were sold, the boys would leave the country and live well.

"Everything went according to plan. The money flowed in. But the boys grew restless. There was little to do between shipments. The friend wandered the countryside and during one of his farthest wanderings he met a young woman. She lived alone and kept goats. He fell in love with her and she with him. He moved in with her.

"The son and his father were worried the friend would reveal the source of his money, but he swore to them he would never tell. When it was time for a shipment, the friend would come to the trailer to help. When the money came, the friend took evening walks out to the road to meet the son. One night, his friend told the son he wanted to marry the girl and make her a partner. The son and his father disagreed with this. They felt such an arrangement would threaten the business.

133

"A compromise had to be found. One night, when the friend went for his usual walk the son brought him to Ashkii's home. They talked over the difficulty but could find no solution. The friend swore he would make sure his girlfriend would never tell anyone else about the business nor would he ask for a larger share. But he could no longer keep it a secret from his future wife.

"The father reluctantly agreed. They all shook hands. But in the son's heart there was anger. Perhaps it was about losing his friend. Perhaps it was about believing this woman would betray them to the authorities or gossip about the artifacts. Whatever it was, the son decided the friend must die.

"Driving home, the friend stepped out of the truck to pee. The son shot him. He drove back and told his father what he had done. They made a plan. The father killed a sheep and mutilated it as a witch might do. Together they drove back to the body and the father, who is skilled in such things, tossed the bloody knife close to the dead man to leave no tracks. Then the son drove his father home and went away. That is the last the father saw his son."

There was quiet in the room for a long time.

"Then you called me to report the sheep mutilation to set up the deception," Jimmy said.

"That is so."

After that, it was clear Ashkii had no more to say. Lané and the two policemen took him into custody. They would take him to Tuba City to be held until a decision regarding jurisdiction could be made. If he was seen as an accomplice to murder, he would become a federal concern.

Zack, Jimmy Chaparral, and Eagle Feather stepped out of Ashkii's house into a dark world, the only illumination the shed light shining its solitary cone. Jimmy latched the door securely behind them. They stood for a moment enjoying the night. There was a breeze that brought with it the pine scent from the upper plateau. Stars twinkled directly overhead but were already diminished by the light of the moon just rising behind the cliff.

"Some trick you pulled with the sheep," Jimmy said to Eagle Feather, admiration in his tone.

"It is an old technique for hunting. I have used it many times to fool deer, but never before to fool a man."

"Where is your truck?"

"It is at the base of the steep road. I coasted without light and left it to approach by foot. The house was dark, I knew there must be trouble."

Eagle Feather turned to look at Zack, who was staring at the cliff top, the moon now fully behind it. He was gazing at the dark figure standing there in silhouette, motionless, looking down on them.

"You see him, don't you," Eagle Feather said.

"Yes, I see him. He is content now."

Eagle Feather gaze was on Zack. He said, "You'll do, White Man. You'll do."

The three turned as one to walk back to their trucks.

EPILOGUE

It was three months before circumstances brought Zack back to Elk Wells. These days he traveled in a different direction having rented a ranch up north near Page. He spent most of his time on the road between the ranch and Tuba City. Today he was on his way to Red Lake on mundane business and decided to stop at Katie's Cafe for a bite and some of her TLC.

Eagle Feather and Jimmy Chaparral were there at a table. They beckoned Zack to join them.

Eagle Feather gave him a long look. "You've changed, White Man. Your skin is brown. You walk with confidence. You almost appear to belong."

"You are not covered in sweat and your shoes are not full of sand," Jimmy said.

"It's nice to see you, too," Zack said with a grin and pulled up a chair. He sat down and waved to Katie. She gave a big smile and brought over coffee.

Jimmy wasn't done with Zack yet. "I'm surprised Bella let you go long enough to drive here."

Zack could feel himself blush. "We're just friends."

"That's not what I'm hearing through the Navajo gossip channels," Jimmy said.

Figuring it was time to change the subject, Zack said, "Did you hear the news about Witherspoon?"

"You mean the FBI man from Flagstaff with the large stick up his butt?" Jimmy asked.

Eagle Feather grinned at Jimmy. "The one who wanted to hang you for the murder of Curtis Peaches."

"That's the one," Zack said.

"What about him?" Jimmy asked.

"Well, I learned this morning he's been fired from the FBI and may be facing felony charges."

Both Navajos stared at Zack.

"What for?" Jimmy asked.

Zack sipped his coffee, enjoying the moment. "There was a reason he tried so hard to pin the murder on Jimmy. After Ashkii's arrest and his story came out, the FBI became involved because of the transportation of stolen goods across state lines, or in this case across international borders. They traced the stolen artifacts to a dealer in Flagstaff who in turn shipped them to a big buyer in Houston, Texas. The Texas man had a lot of expensive clients who paid top dollar for rare artifacts and relics. The FBI was able to close down the Texas business, then took a long look at how the Flagstaff guy had managed to stay under the radar."

Katie arrived to take Zack's order. He pretended to vacillate between two choices just to stretch the moment. Both Navajo stared at him with stone faces.

When Katie finally left to prepare his food, Zack grinned at his friends and continued. "Well, they found the Flagstaff dealer had been paying off some local policemen to leave him alone. Agent Witherspoon was with the FBI task force that went to arrest the cops. The cops pointed the finger at Witherspoon. It seems he had been lining his shelves with some rare artifacts in exchange for sheltering the operation from federal scrutiny."

Zack sat back and grinned at his friends. "What do you think about that?"

"It couldn't have happened to a nicer guy," Jimmy said.

"I never liked the man," Eagle Feather said.

137

Jimmy pushed some food around on his plate with his fork. "It's too bad about Ashkii."

Zack raised his eyebrows. "I thought that worked out well for him. The FBI left him to the Navajo Justice system, and they slapped him with a big fine, right?"

Jimmy glanced at Zack. "Not exactly. He was sentenced for two major crimes, stealing from the Navajo Nation for personal profit and aiding in covering up a murder. His sentences were consecutive. He was given a large fine, which he could not pay. He was incarcerated, which in this case meant working for the tribe eight hours a day for ten years. But the sentence that really hurt was the shaming, where he was made to wear a sign at all times designating him as an offender."

"That is the punishment that hurt him too much," Eagle Feather said.

"Too much?" Zack asked.

"He committed suicide," Jimmy said. "They found him hanging from the roof beam in his hogan."

"Damn. In his heart, he was a good man," Zack said.

The Navajos nodded. No one spoke.

Katie hustled over, her features exuding her usual cheer and good humor. "Anything else, gentlemen? We've got fresh apple pie. I can heat some up for you."

The three chairs scraped back as the men stood.

"Oh, no, I've eaten too much already," Jimmy said.

"I must meet my clients at the airport," Eagle Feather said.

"I've got to be on my way," Zack said.

The three stepped out onto the boardwalk and stood together for a moment. The sun shone bright, the sky was azure blue with white puff clouds, a dog barked somewhere, the scent of fresh baked bread swirled about, cheery music sounded from a shop down the street. It was the start of another day in Navajo Land.

Also By R Lawson Gamble

ZACK TOLLIVER, FBI, MYSTERY SERIES

THE OTHER

MESTACLOCAN

ZACA

CAT

UNDER DESERT SAND

CANAAN'S SECRET

ABOUT THE AUTHOR

R Lawson Gamble enjoys the Southwest, great stories, Indian lore and culture, and scary paranormal possibilities, all of which find their way into the *ZACK TOLLIVER, FBI* series of novels. The author lives in Los Alamos, California among the beautiful Central Coast Golden Hills.

Editing a book is a tedious and not always successful task, even for professionals. You, the reader, are the final bastion. If you have found errors in this book and are willing to email me (rlawsongamble@gmail.com) with the error and its location, I will be grateful. Thank you.

Thank you for purchasing THE DARK ROAD. I know you could have picked any number of books to read, but you picked this book and for that I am grateful.

I hope you found it enjoyable. If so, please consider sharing this book with your friends and family by posting to Facebook and Twitter . I'd also enjoy hearing from you and hope you might take some time to post a review on Amazon. Your feedback and support will help this author improve his writing craft for future projects.

Happy Reading!

Made in the USA
Columbia, SC
04 April 2019